She couldn't stop

The last time she'd seen ~~~~~~~~~~~~~~~~~~~~~~~~~~~ were both on the cusp of teenhood. Still kids.

He looked exactly the same, but somehow different in so many different ways—subtle and obvious—that were near impossible to process all at once. The reassuring brown of his irises and the slight hook of his Roman nose remained. But his wavy hair was much longer now, the ends finishing at the nape of his neck and curling outward, giving him a regal sort of charm.

Same was their difference in height. She must have had about two inches on him—even more so with her platform shoes on.

New was the lean edge to his build. A thin chain necklace took residence midway down his chest, the sun's glare and the half-buttoned state of his short-sleeved shirt attracting her attention downward.

An embarrassed flush wormed its way through Damica's body as he drank in her changed appearance with the same interest.

PRINCE'S REUNION IN PARADISE

FAYE ACHEAMPONG

ROMANCE

**Harlequin®
ROMANCE**

ISBN-13: 978-1-335-21623-6

Prince's Reunion in Paradise

Recycling programs
for this product may
not exist in your area.

 Harlequin Enterprises ULC
22 Adelaide St. West, 41st Floor
Toronto, Ontario M5H 4E3, Canada
www.Harlequin.com

Printed in U.S.A.

Faye Acheampong's journey as a romance author began in 2015, when she shared her creative writing online out of boredom. She has also experimented with playwriting, screenwriting and written role-play and is always searching for ways to expand her love of storytelling. In 2022, she was announced as the winner of Harlequin's Love to Write Competition, hosted in partnership with Amber Rose Gill. Faye lives in London but regularly daydreams about moving elsewhere. Visit fayeacheampong.com to find out more. You can also follow Faye on Instagram @fayeacheampong and X @fayeursoquiet.

Also by Faye Acheampong

Harlequin Romance

The Christmas That Changed Everything

Visit the Author Profile page at Harlequin.com.

PROLOGUE

THIRTEEN-YEAR-OLD DAMICA FOYE studied the Dani DoRight doll, unsure about whether she wanted to cradle the plastic toy human in her arms or rip its entire head off.

She's not me. I'm not her, she chanted to herself again and again.

For a handful of imaginary handclaps Damica forgot about the aroma of cleaning chemicals and the silent city of shaggy mopheads, surface cleaner bottles and supply carts surrounding her. The new song she'd accidentally made up was a welcome distraction from the unexpected misery that came with playing one of the most recognisable fictional characters in the world. She'd become so recognisable that she preferred to hide.

The door guarding the conference building's maintenance closet betrayed her, opening with a trespassing click. Reflexively, Damica's hand flew up to protect her face from the cameras and she braced herself for a tidal wave of barks.

'Smile Dani!'

'Over here, Dani!'

'Put your hands on your hips, Dani—not both, just the one.'

'Look over here—at me only, sweetheart, forget the others.'

Instead, she was cowering away from a solitary silhouette in the non-threatening brightness of the hallway.

A…boy? Shorter than her. With dark wavy hair and bronze-coloured skin. He appeared to be around her age, but the confident style and cut of his suit suggested he was cosplaying someone more mature. The shock in the width of his brown eyes outdid Damica's astonishment.

She was actually relieved.

The event photographers or, worse, her mom, hadn't found her yet.

Only Prince Dorian of Concarre.

'This hiding spot is taken!' Damica squeaked, sticking her head out of the unlit space to peep left and right.

The coast was clear. For now. She wondered if she should be bowing or offering him a handshake—that was how everyone else at the Youth Today, Leaders Tomorrow conference had reacted to his presence.

'Pick another… Your Highness.'

That sounded polite enough, didn't it?

The Prince peered past her, inside the dark otherworld of the cleaners' closet. He took in the nozzles protruding from the spray bottles and the exhausted aprons hanging from their hooks like ghouls.

Authority overrode the confusion of his round face and the unbroken pitch of his voice. 'There seems to be plenty of room.'

'No, there isn't.' Damica shook her head stubbornly.

He crossed his arms. 'Yes, there is—'

An army of walkie-talkie beeps and serious codewords echoed in the distance. Bodyguards searching for the young royal who had escaped their watchful eye.

The children were immediately united in their terror. Their disagreement was replaced with the common dance of hopping frantically from foot to foot and a wild choreography of gestures that included repeatedly jabbing a finger over their mouths.

Panic took over as Damica dumped her doll into the nearest bucket, then grabbed Dorian by the lapels of his suit jacket. Pulling him inside the cleaners' closet, she ignored his triumphant smile.

'See, I told you there was room…'

'Shh!'

They were cloaked by darkness once Damica had closed the door as quietly as possible. She put her ear to the surface, listening for the sound of footsteps coming from the other side. Nothing. Crisis averted. Phew!

Suddenly she was bathed in unwelcome light. The closet's flickering lightbulb managed to come alive at the command of the pull switch now manned by Dorian. With a sigh, Damica tugged the string so that the light was turned off.

The Prince turned it on again.

Off. On. *Off.*

Finally he got the message and the safety of the shadows remained uninterrupted.

'Wow…this really looks like you.'

She turned around to see Prince Dorian holding the Dani DoRight doll, squinting at its form.

That was another reason Damica was so comfortable with the closet's dim interior—she didn't have to deal with how dumb and toddlerish her clothes looked. Frowning down at her tutu, jeans and ballet flats, she longed for a more stylish outfit. She wanted to try make-up and high heels and mini-skirts like regular thirteen-year-olds did.

Self-consciously, Damica shrugged. 'Not really. She's not me. My name's not even Dani… it's *Damica*. With an M and a C.'

The nothingness that followed only made her feel more awkward. He wouldn't understand anyway. He was a prince. Royal people probably got to do and wear whatever they wanted to.

She looked up, her gaze connecting with

Dorian's. He watched her as if he could see her clearly.

'I wish I had another name,' he confessed, looking as lost as he sounded. 'People think they know me because they've heard of me. I don't get to introduce myself. It's weird.'

'Having two names is overrated, so you're not missing out on anything. No one cares about the real me any more…they're only interested in the new version,' she told him, surprising herself with her own honesty.

Slowly Damica sank onto the floor, sitting down cross-legged and leaning back against the chilly brick wall. Dorian joined the descent, settling with his legs straight. She observed him tapping the heels of his smart-looking shoes together, so the leather clapped, creating a tune.

'Choose one,' she said.

He paused. 'Pardon?'

'A new name.'

Being alone with him wasn't so bad, she decided. They were more similar than she'd thought.

'Oh.' His posture straightened whilst his fingers plucked at the air, as if he was concentrating hard on conjuring up a… 'Wilbur.'

Damica snorted. She slapped a hand over her mouth, but that did little to stop the giggle fizzing up inside her.

'What?' Dorian demanded. 'What's wrong with Wilbur?'

She scrunched up her nose. 'It's so—I dunno—*old*!'

'Pick something that suits me, then.' He'd deflated into a relaxed state instead of a sad one.

'Okay. You look like a…' Damica cleared her throat and pumped her fists to add some pizzazz. 'Romeo!'

He laughed. 'No, I do not.'

'You do!'

And that was that. They were familiar enough to banter with each other…share feelings that were supposed to go unspoken about and ask questions that usually fell upon deaf ears.

Damica didn't know if she'd spent twenty minutes talking with Dorian or several hours. What mattered most was that this was the most fun she'd had at Youth Today, Leaders Tomorrow and she wanted it to last longer. By the time his security team raided the haven of the cleaners' closet she'd opened up about how she was scared her mom cared more about the Feir Channel pay-cheques than her.

In return, Dorian had confided in her about how he missed his dad a lot, and was only able to get his attention by pretending to be 'macho'.

One of Dorian's guards escorted Damica back to where her mom was pacing around like a headless chicken. Just as Damica had predicted, she was greeted with a scolding lecture about setting a bad example and the whereabouts of the lost doll before the conference's scheduled presentations continued for the day.

Somewhere between the interpretative dance promoting wildlife conservation and the speech about running for Youth World Government, the kid next to her nudged her shoulder and dropped a folded sheet of lined paper clipped to a ballpoint pen on her lap. The message was addressed to her, however she didn't recognise the penmanship.

Damica scanned the hall, packed with child activists, musical prodigies, young royals and teen starlets, until she detected Dorian seated at the very opposite end of her row. He sent her a shy wave and pointed at the message he'd sent out into the sea of attendees.

She grinned back, then read the contents of her delivery:

Do you have email?
From...maybe Giorgios???

Damica hadn't got to say goodbye to him before, when they'd been so harshly separated, and she'd accepted that they would never meet again and trusted that her secrets would be safe with him. Now, shimmering with hope, she realised that she and Dorian would never truly be apart from each other if they became pen pals.

She freed the pen, pressed down the button and started to write her email address...

Age Thirteen

From: mrdoryfish7@inbox.com
To: damidiamondzzz@inbox.com
Subject: READ ME... IT'S URGENT!!

Hi :D

From: damidiamondzzz@inbox.com
To: mrdoryfish7@inbox.com
Re: READ ME... IT'S URGENT!!

Hello!!

PS Did you get the email chain I sent to you? Who did you forward it to?

PPS Is your email name coz of *Finding Nemo*? I had to go to the premiere... Premieres suck! I hate it when the men with cameras shout at me...

From: mrdoryfish7@inbox.com
to: damidiamondzzz@inbox.com
Subject: READ ME... IT'S URGENT!!

Um... I'm not going to tell you that! Don't want seven years bad luck!

Try hiding from them again? They can't take pictures if they can't see you.

When I'm travelling I sometimes lie down in the car boot. Works every time!

:D

CHAPTER ONE

Twenty years later

THE FIRST RULE of looking after a child: do not lose said child.

Damica was already off to a terrible start.

The soles of her platform flip-flops thwacked against the stone ground, rivalling the hammering of her speeding heart, during the frantic search of her nephew. She'd looked away for literally *a minute*, assuming Jalen would be fine whilst she brought him a cone from the counter at the resort's ice cream parlour. However, she was now paying the price for underestimating the four-year-old boy's energetic streak and thirst for adventure.

He'd taken his auntie's lack of supervision as an opportunity to dash out of the parlour and explore the resort all on his own.

Under prolonged exposure to the Maldivian afternoon sun, the once chilled scoop of mint and milk chocolate ice cream was now a pathetic green-brown blob. Streams of melted ice cream oozed down the softening wafer cone and onto Damica's hand, causing her to pull a face. Sighing, she slowed down to dump the dying delicacy into a nearby bin and shake away the mess.

How could she call herself a functioning adult when she couldn't even handle the responsibility of caring for her own nephew?

Immature. Selfish. Irresponsible—

Damica closed her eyes and ran through the breathing exercises introduced to her by her therapist.

Inhale for four seconds, hold for seven seconds, exhale for eight.

You're free now, she reminded herself.

Her Dani DoRight days were long behind her, as was the overwhelming control of her mother. Plus, Damica had fulfilled all contractual obligations to her record label and concluded her music career with a worldwide tour just five months earlier. This holiday in the Maldives with her close family was way overdue. At long last she was free. Life was good. Normality was all she'd ever wanted.

She stood up straighter and readjusted the dark lenses of her designer sunglasses. There was no time to enjoy the summer heat, the crisp cerulean blue sky and salty sea air. And there was even less time to care about the passing vacationers—friends, families and couples—who reacted to the white patches on her brown skin with typical quizzical glances.

Damica focused on scrutinising the picturesque landscape of the Étoile Privée Resort. The path before her branched off at consistent intervals, leading to the elated squeals and chlorinated turquoise rush of the water park, or the contemplative silence of the resort boutique. Down on the beach, the members of a yoga class executed poses with such stillness that they might have been mistaken for a collection of statues parked on the vastness of the golden sand.

No sign of Jalen, though.

She'd already checked the marina, the fitness centre and the reception building to no avail.

Damica prayed that Jalen was at least still on the main island, and wasn't sobbing in the jungle area with a scraped and bloody knee—or, worse, floating face-down in the sea…

Fear and gut feeling guided Damica straight ahead, towards the sharp architecture of the ocean-front villas, which were bisected by a wood-planked pier that seemed to stretch on for ever. Explaining to her younger sister Taylor and her brother-in-law that she'd lost their only child wasn't an option.

The slap of Damica's flip-flops fired up again, and her sundress swished around her legs as she moved with purpose. Pumping adrenaline made her all the more aware of her surroundings: of the cool shadows of the looming palm trees growing sparser as she approached the water. Of the faraway trilling of a bicycle bell followed by sombre calls to be careful. Then, unfiltered boyish laughter that was instantly identifiable.

'Jalen?' Damica shouted at the blurry figures cruising in her direction along the wooden walkway.

Someone on a bike, and a person jogging behind, struggling to keep up. From a distance, she was able to pinpoint her nephew. He was having the time of his life, sitting on the wicker basket fixed to the cycle's handlebars.

'Jalen, there you…!'

The projection of her voice fell when the cyclist's features came into clear view.

Dorian Saadoun Sotiropoulos.

The joyous shine vacated Dorian's facial expression and alarm invaded once he saw Damica. Taken with equal shock, his hold on the bike slackened and it toppled from side to side. Jalen screeched in excitement, clinging to the basket for dear life as he mistook Dorian's action for an added thrill to the ride experience.

The chaser's thudding footsteps decelerated as he neared. Heavy hands protectively landed on the Prince's shoulder and the bicycle saddle just as Dorian planted a shaky foot on the ground.

Despite drowning in sweat and the self-inflicted

furnace generated by his all-black attire, the body-guard muttered stoically, 'Careful, Your Highness.'

'Thank you, Ravi.' Dorian's eyes refused to part from Damica as he spoke.

She couldn't stop observing him either.

The last time she'd seen him in person had been when they were both on the cusp of teen hood. Still kids.

He looked exactly the same, but somehow different. In so many different ways—subtle and obvious—that it was near-impossible to process them all at once. The reassuring brown of his irises and the slight hook of his Roman nose remained. But his wavy hair was much longer now, the ends finishing at the nape of his neck and curling outward, giving him a regal sort of charm.

Their difference in height was the same. She must have had about two inches on him—even more so with her platform shoes on.

New was the lean edge to his build. A thin chain necklace had residence midway down his chest, the sun's glare and the half-buttoned state of his short-sleeved shirt attracted her attention downward.

An embarrassed flush wormed its way through Damica's body as he drank in her changed appearance with the same interest. On the tip of her tongue, a joke about Dorian finally sprouting the chest hair his father had so badly wanted him to have immediately formed. However, she knew that its delivery would only make this reunion more tense.

She recalled the finality of their last email exchange. How she'd obviously no longer had a place within the strict, regulated boundaries of his life. Damica hadn't realised at the time, but the abrupt end of their friendship had been the best outcome for them both. In hindsight, their falling out seemed like a juvenile case of miscommunication. Nonetheless, the overarching message had been that they were heading for very different trajectories in life.

Dorian was destined to be the sovereign ruler of Concarre—a small but prosperous nation situated in the Mediterranean Sea, midway between southern Greece and Egypt. Polite behaviour, sacrifice and protocol were on the cards for him.

As for Damica…it would be a cold day in hell before she relinquished control to another person or a greater cause again.

'Again! Again! Again!'

Jalen's chanting faded in, breaking up the pair's deep study of one another.

'No. You've had enough fun today.'

Damica charged up to the bicycle and lifted her nephew out of the large basket. After his small feet were reunited with the wooden planks of the pier, she crouched down so they were eye to eye. She cupped his cheeks, making sure to keep her hold gentle but firm as he whined and attempted to wriggle away from accountability. His features—a healthy head of tight curls, expressive eyes that creased at the corners and a round face—were the perfect summarisation of Taylor and her husband Leroy.

'You almost gave me a heart attack. Don't run off like that again.'

Judging by the way Jalen stilled and looked down shamefully, she'd perfected her 'mommy voice'. No sense of pride completed this victory, though. Only a building nervousness as Dorian closely watched the exchange, his stare clinging to Damica like a second skin.

She wrapped a hand around one of Jalen's and stood up again. Checking that she was still protected by the dark lenses of her eyewear, Damica pulled on a false mask of indifference.

'What are you doing here?' she asked Dorian, not meaning to sound as breathless as she felt.

Her efforts were ultimately in vain. She would have blamed the weather, but she'd always preferred hotter climates.

'Taking a sabbatical.'

Dorian dismounted from the bicycle, smoothly swinging his leg over the seat. Quickly, he handed over the two-wheeled vehicle to his bodyguard, so he could allocate all his attention to Damica and Jalen.

'And you?'

'Family holiday.'

The less she said the better. She couldn't embarrass herself further that way.

Nine years had passed since she'd last heard from Dorian. Almost a decade. Damica had assumed the wound of their separation was well and truly healed. But something as simple as their contrast in motives for their stay here caused the resurfacing of a tender soreness that was too familiar. Even the way Dorian strode undecidedly towards her and Jalen, whilst the bodyguard shadowed him, informed Damica that a restoration of their previous relationship would be impossible.

She could forgive him if she wanted to…but forgetting about their clashing principles? Unlikely.

'How…how are you?' Dorian's focal point jumped between her blank face—she was working overtime to give nothing away—and Jalen, who was restlessly tugging on her arm.

She dodged the question entirely and pivoted. 'Where did you find him?'

'Here. Running up and down.'

To demonstrate, Dorian pointed down the stretch of the jetty and made his fingers sprint through the air.

'Initially, I didn't want to interrupt—he said

he was hiding from his aunt, so I assumed there was a game of hide-and-seek happening. But then he got distracted by my bike.'

Damica was temporarily lulled by Dorian's version of events. A distinct accent still underscored his words. However, his tone had matured considerably into a deep, engaging articulation. The boy from the janitor's closet was long gone.

As she noticed the stubble framing his mouth, Damica wondered if he was still obsessed with poetry. She remembered the essay's worth of emails he'd sent her from his boarding school library, chronicling his analyses…

Stop.

'We were about to take him to the concierge desk,' Dorian concluded, utterly oblivious to her slipping resolve. He regarded Jalen with fond confusion. 'Is he your…?'

'Nephew?' She finished off the sentence, watching inexplicable relief, hurt and then guilt play across his demeanour. 'Yes,' she added quietly.

Huh? Had Dorian thought Jalen was her son? If so, his reaction didn't make any sense. She hadn't been attached to any pregnancy rumours since she was a teenager, and keeping a child secret from the press would be highly unrealistic.

Clearly it was just she who checked the tabloids occasionally, to see how he was doing, knowing full well that the updates would be inaccurate. But something was better than nothing. Although now she could see it had been a useless venture.

As if sensing the uncertain shift in energy, Dorian furrowed his brow in regret. 'Damica—'

'Say *thank you* to Dorian and his friend.'

She ushered Jalen in front of her and positioned both hands defensively on his shoulders. The source of Dorian's sadness was none of her business. Discussing feelings was something friends—which they no longer were—did.

'Thank you, Dorian's friend! Thank you, Dorian!' Jalen waved enthusiastically at the Prince and his bodyguard, garnering a respectful nod from them both.

Dorian raised his palm, inviting the young boy to give him a high five. With no delay, Jalen reached up to slap the surface of his hand against Dorian's. The variance in size and the affectionate curve of Dorian's smile triggered a squeezing sensation between Damica's lungs.

Clearing her throat, she announced, 'Let's go…'

She pulled Jalen away, directing him back towards the main island. He whinged in protest, but eventually conformed.

They were still within earshot of Dorian's closing comment. 'Nice to see you again.'

An itch pierced between her shoulder blades

before dipping lower. Damica could feel him contemplating her retreating back, but she feigned ignorance. Believably too.

The impulse to return to Dorian lessened with the growing distance. As she and Jalen walked back together she made sure to swing their joined hands, to keep him entertained. Jalen beamed at the motion, falling for the distraction. And so did Damica for a short while.

The Étoile Privée Resort website boasted that its twenty-two-acre grounds in the Maldives were optimal for high-profile guests who desired privacy. Damica prayed that she would in future experience the full extent of this geography, and blamed her reunion with Dorian on mere coincidence. The probability of them running into each other again was zero. This holiday was designed for her to reclaim her free time, bond with Jalen and figure out who exactly she was outside of being a world-famous entertainer.

She'd already missed out on so many milestones due to work. The summer ahead would be dedicated to what mattered most: creating new memories and reconnecting with her identity.

Whatever that was.

Nothing and no one would get in the way of that. She'd make sure of it.

Age Twenty-Four

From: damidiamondzzz@inbox.com
To: mrdoryfish7@inbox.com
Subject: Sorry and Save the Date!

Dorian,
Hey! how have you been lately?

Sorry that it's been so long since my last email. Between all the music video shoots, photoshoots, meetings and recording sessions, it's like I barely have a life any more.

But that will all change tomorrow night—maybe the evening on the day after. The date hasn't been finalised!

Me and Zak are getting married! In Vegas!

We want the affair to be super-small and intimate, so only our close friends are invited. That includes you. It would mean everything to me to have you present at my wedding. You've been one of my best friends for so long, and I love you so much, so it's a no-brainer that you're getting this email.

Diana is more than welcome to join us too. I can't wait to finally meet her, and to actually see you in front of me! This has been a long time in the making...

Seeing as I'm both the bride and the wedding

planner, I'll accept your response as your RSVP, or whatever they are called. LOL!

Love ya!

Dami xo

From: mrdoryfish7@inbox.com
To: damidiamondzzz@inbox.com
Re: Sorry and Save the Date!

Hello, Damica,

I'm well. It's nice to hear from you again.

I regret to inform you that I will not be able to attend the ceremony in Vegas. Although I am currently on leave from any royal duties, it would be most inconvenient for me to travel out of the country at such short notice. My foundation, the people of Concarre, my future wife and children—whoever they may be—need me, and it is my responsibility to serve them to the best of my ability.

Many congratulations on your engagement to Zak. I hope you have a happy marriage.

Best,

Dorian

From: damidiamondzzz@inbox.com
To: mrdoryfish7@inbox.com
Re: Sorry and Save the Date!

Aw, boo!

I know I shouldn't push you to change your

mind, but…this is me, pushing you to change your mind!

This is basically the first time in for ever that our schedules are matching up and you're choosing to stay home?

Think of all the Elvis impersonators, alcohol and cake you'll miss out on. Even better, think of the wild story you'll get to tell your kids when you tuck them in at night, years from now. You've gotta prove to them that their daddy wasn't boring!

What went down in the last seven months?

I know this is all super last-minute, but me and Zak will pay for everything, so don't worry about the cost. Just get over here.

Dami

PS Cake depends on whether there are any cake stores around that can finish our order within such a short turnaround.

From: mrdoryfish7@inbox.com
To: damidiamondzzz@inbox.com
Re: Sorry and Save the Date!

I'd rather not delve into any specifics, but Diana and I have mutually agreed to part ways. During this time I have come to treasure the work I do with CYAF, no matter how strenuous it may be—this may come as a surprise to you, considering your disdain for most work.

Now that I am actively crafting a legacy of my

own, I realise that sacrifice comes along with the construction of something far greater than myself. Unfortunately, missing your ceremony is a part of this sacrifice.

Please try to understand this.

From: damidiamondzzz@inbox.com
To: mrdoryfish7@inbox.com
Re: Sorry and Save the Date!

Don't preach to me about the meaning of hard work, Dorian. Whatever you get up to at your vanity project isn't the same as working twelve-hour days as a child, and dancing so hard you have blisters on your feet.

If I wanna 'sacrifice' everything and put myself first for just one night, I will.

From: mrdoryfish7@inbox.com
To: damidiamondzzz@inbox.com
Re: Sorry and Save the Date!

I take it your mother has no knowledge of your plans? Doesn't she hate Zachary? I mean... I thought you caught him going through your wallet last year.

From: damidiamondzzz@inbox.com
To: mrdoryfish7@inbox.com
Re: Sorry and Save the Date!

That was a misunderstanding!!!

I don't care what either of you think. I sleep with who I want, orgasm as much as I want, show as much skin as I want. And I'll continue to do what I want.

From: mrdoryfish7@inbox.com
To: damidiamondzzz@inbox.com
Re: Sorry and Save the Date!

The last thing I want to do is control you. All I'm doing is advising you to think before making such a rash decision.

From: damidiamondzzz@inbox.com
To: mrdoryfish7@inbox.com
Re: Sorry and Save the Date!

Well, if the options are being Daddy's little puppet, like you, or a reckless mess, I know which one I'm choosing!
    :)

From: mrdoryfish7@inbox.com
To: damidiamondzzz@inbox.com
Re: Sorry and Save the Date!

Have a nice life, Damica. Don't bother to come crying to me when Zak reveals himself to be the lowlife he's already shown himself to be.

Not every sensible decision exists to be an inconvenience to you.

From: mrdoryfish7@inbox.com
To: damidiamondzzz@inbox.com
Subject: About Yesterday...

Damica,
I apologise for the comments I made previously. Tension was running high, and we've both experienced a world of change since we spoke last.

Perhaps it would be beneficial to discuss everything in a video call? What time of the day would work best for you?

Yours,
Dorian

CHAPTER TWO

DESPITE FINDING THE phrase 'Heavy is the head that wears the crown' incredibly unoriginal, its sentiment rang painfully true for Dorian Saadoun Sotiropoulos.

As evening shrouded the paradisiacal resort, the Crown Prince of Concarre strolled through one of the four restaurants on site. The name of this particular eatery evaded his mind, nonetheless its modern décor and bespoke menu, specialising in the finest Japanese and East Asian cuisine, had left a lasting impression on his senses.

Melancholy occupied the space beside him like an invisible companion, prompting him to remember that he had no one to share this experience with. He wanted to count Ravi as a sort of travel buddy, but the bodyguard was a stickler for formalities. And procedure dictated that the professional boundaries between security staff and the Concarri royal family were uncrossable.

The Prince sighed to himself, breathing in the

idle clink of cutlery against ceramics and the inviting aromas wafting from the open counter in the process. Kanou-style paintings lined the walls, along with leather booths accommodating several other guests. In a far corner sat none other than Damica and her nephew.

Dorian changed course immediately, sidestepping to seek refuge behind a potted plant.

Fortunately, she hadn't spotted him.

Jalen was fussing with his ketchup-stained napkin, and Damica was busy using a knife and fork to cut up katsu chicken into digestible pieces for him. The scene was an instant hit of dopamine, helping Dorian to escape the sobering aspects of his life.

A polite tap on his shoulder made him flinch.

'Do you still intend to dine here, Your Highness?' Ravi enquired discreetly.

Dorian's response was an unbothered wave. The private dining room and all those empty chairs could wait.

In his head, he cursed at how suspicious he appeared in his current predicament. No better than the paparazzi who routinely camped out in the bushes neighbouring the palace back home.

He still couldn't quite believe that he and Damica had crossed paths again. Once had been luck. Maybe twice was a sign that they were supposed to reconcile?

The aftermath of their fallout had stalked him

into his late twenties and beyond. The morning after their heated email exchange had consisted of him refreshing his inbox every hour, on the hour. He had no idea whether she'd read his last message and deliberately ignored him thereafter, or if she'd simply stopped visiting her email account altogether after he'd essentially ended their friendship.

The mysterious way she'd conducted herself during their latest interaction had confirmed little, leaving him with no other option but to revisit the event under the precision of a magnifying glass. Now it was painfully easy to lose himself in the elegant slope of her neck, and the way she scrunched up her nose ever so slightly...

Self-inflicted suffering wasn't really Dorian's style, but the dull twinge awakened by Jalen was worth it. Dorian loved children. Mandatory school visits had always been the highlight of his duties. He adored the simplicity with which children viewed the world, and their lack of shame. Kids were beacons of creativity and playfulness and he'd always be willing to tend the flames of that.

Perhaps his negative experiences with his own father had spawned Dorian's wishes to be a parent himself, so he could right all those wrongs. Before receiving devastating news from the royal household physician Dorian had eagerly anticipated the day he'd become a dad. Now burdened with the knowledge of abnormalities in his sperm's shape, he was questioning if that blessing would ever arise.

And, if it did, would he be co-parenting with a woman who was genuinely attracted to him in spite of his shortcomings in fertility?

Digging around in the pockets of his shorts, Dorian sought catharsis in the form of a toothpick. Typically, he'd light a cigarette. But habitual smoking was likely the cause of his problems 'downstairs', so he'd had to retire that pastime for good.

Dorian's hand resurfaced empty: he must have left the toothpick box in his villa.

Determined not to drown in his issues, he ventured out of his hiding spot and drifted towards the booth Damica and her nephew were seated in. With Ravi on his tail, Dorian did his best to keep his stride casual. Once he reached the table, he hovered at its edge, suddenly grappling with his own awkwardness.

Jalen perked up and his bright inquisitiveness greeted Dorian like an old friend. Simultaneously, Damica's quiet acknowledgment of him—and Ravi—was tinged with caution. Dorian second-guessed his intentions in coming over. The inexplicable pull that had directed him to her side wasn't something he could voice without sounding over-familiar. They weren't children and nor were they friends any more.

'Good evening…'

To buy himself enough time to come up with a believable excuse for his intrusion, he gesticulated at the half-eaten dishes on the tabletop. Their dinner. The private dining room included in his resort package became a useful asset all of a sudden.

'I'm about to have my evening meal and I was hoping you would join me.'

Gasping in excitement, Jalen placed his fork down and began scooting out of the booth.

'Jalen, sit still, please,' Damica ordered.

'If you'd like to, of course,' Dorian added hastily, taking note of the exhaustion marking her tone. 'I'll understand if not.'

He looked to her for final approval, and was pleasantly surprised to find a ghost of a smile waltzing across her lips. Under his inspection, she squashed it with stolidness, narrowing her eyes at him as if she could tell he was improvising. Which he was.

'Can we, Auntie Dami?' Jalen pleaded. 'Please, please, please, please?'

'Hmm…fine,' she agreed, still avoiding eye contact with Dorian.

He was glad her eyes weren't concealed by her sunglasses this time around—the almond shape, upturned corners and haunting shade of brown were just as he remembered them.

Unhurriedly, Damica got to her feet and selected a few plates to take with her. Dorian rushed to provide his assistance, discerning the scent of cocoa butter lotion and rose perfume scent in the midst of picking up whichever dishes she pointed to.

With renewed optimism about his scheduled getaway, he broke away to lead the small group to his private dining spot.

They resettled at the long rectangular table in the dining room booked for Dorian. Ravi blended into the background, taking up a post by the door, sacrificing comfort and a hot meal for optimum viewing of all the space's exits and entrances whilst the staff finished serving up a banquet's worth of food.

Jalen dug in, paying no mind to the rising steam. A glass wall revealed the setting sun bleeding across the sky in various hues of orange, yellow and pinks. Having already become accustomed to the view, Dorian observed Damica admiring the Maldivian evening sky with unrestrained awe.

The innocence of her expression transported him back to their first meeting at thirteen years old. And he still prided himself on being able to grant her freedom—all three seconds of it— from the way they'd both been losing their entire childhoods to adult responsibilities.

The moment ended swiftly.

Realising she was under the microscope of

his surveillance, Damica stiffened and quickly sought diversion in teaching Jalen how to blow on his food to cool it down. The shift in her body language jogged Dorian's memory of how she didn't care for being stared at. Attracting attention was a phenomenon that predated Damica's rise to fame. In their emails, she'd opened up considerably about living with vitiligo since the age of four.

Although her autoimmune condition wasn't the subject of his current musing, Dorian was apologetic. Redirecting his focus to his own choice of meal—Thai fish cakes with sweet chilli sauce—he raced through the contents of his mind for a conversation-starter that would bridge the gaping silence between them.

He flattened the impulse to admit aloud that he'd been overjoyed by the reports that she'd annulled her marriage to that opportunistic fool whose name hadn't been worth remembering.

Dorian glanced at Jalen, who was happily munching away on some Peking duck pancakes.

Definitely not. Any contributing factors to the demise of his and Damica's friendship would best be spoken of in private. Plus, any comment on her relationship history would expose the fact that he'd read numerous articles about her over the years—which was hardly a step above his current behaviour: gawking at her as if she was a restored Michelangelo painting.

So much for being better than a creepy photojournalist...

Instead, he opted for a safe, inoffensive topic that surely he couldn't go wrong with. 'Congratulations on your retirement.'

Damica took her time before replying, chewing on the last of her vegetable spring rolls. The soundless grind of her teeth outdid the anticipation of any regular countdown, and it was during this suspense that Dorian realised he'd in fact unveiled his awareness of her presence in international news. Although her exit from the music industry had made headlines all over the world, so he could still feign casualness if needed.

She swallowed, drawing him back to the point of her chin and the bobbing of her throat. 'Thank you... I...er...' Grabbing the large serving spoon protruding from the closest bowl of sticky rice, she gave herself another helping. 'Sorry to hear about your engagement.'

She waved the utensil towards his near-empty plate. Spoon or olive branch? Regardless, Dorian was intent on turning this drop of conversation into a bucketful. Her mumbled answer also suggested his online stalking wasn't one-sided.

Dorian nudged his plate over, sounding happier than one might assume a heartbroken bachelor would as he said, 'Thank you.'

Damica raised an eyebrow.

'Convenient arrangement,' Dorian explained. 'Ultimately, we worked better as friends.'

Sophie was the type of woman that everyone expected him to marry: private-school-and-university-educated like himself, someone who ran in aristocratic circles, was experienced in charity work. Their friendship with 'benefits' had made matters easier too—they'd skipped the whole getting-to-know-each-other charade. They'd made each other happy enough. Intercourse had been satisfying enough. The public reception they'd received had been good enough.

For men like Dorian, romantic love would always be nothing but a fairytale. Archaic tradition dictated that all marrying royals had to undergo fertility testing, to check that they would be able to continue the line of succession. Dorian's results may as well have read 'failure', because that was how he'd felt. When the time had come to involve Sophie in his discovery...he'd choked. He hadn't been able to bear the thought of her, or any more people, knowing what he was.

Blaming his decision on something nonsensical, he'd ended their engagement. She hadn't been particularly devastated. Concarre had briefly mourned the death of 'Dophie' and taken the royal communications office's lie-infested statement as the truth.

Dorian would have thrown himself into his royal duties with full force afterwards, to assure himself that he could still serve the Kingdom of Concarre, but the test results had called his ability to provide an heir into question.

'I'm guessing your father wasn't pleased?' Damica tapped the spoon against Dorian's plate, depositing a scoop of rice.

They both gritted their teeth at the mention of Concarre's reigning king. Dismay eclipsed Dorian's elation over Damica's lowering guard. Luckily, his father had not been privy to the test results. To avoid a brutal attack on his masculinity, Dorian had omitted the real reason for the breakup during the King's interrogation.

When in Concarre, do as the royal family always does: hop on a plane to the Maldives, to avoid further discussion with your father.

Shaking his head, Dorian recounted, 'I think he broke the world record for the highest usage of the word "coward" in a single conversation.'

'Yikes.' Damica continued eating.

'In retrospect, it could be argued that he wanted to marry Sophie more than I did.'

Dorian paused to wolf down a portion of his meal and wash it down with some wine. Over the rim of his glass, he gently posed a question.

'How did your mother react to your news?'

'We haven't spoken since she stopped managing me.'

The hurt flashing across Damica's features,

contradicted the indifferent rise and drop of her shoulders.

'My sister's tried passing on a few messages for me, but I never get a response…'

She inhaled, as if preparing to spill more. But the further outpouring of emotion never came.

Protectiveness stirred inside him like a beast evaluating whether or not to pounce on an invader.

'Don't let her ruin this,' he said. 'I know this— it's what you've always wanted.'

'It doesn't feel like I thought it would. It's like…' Damica's head tilted from left to right, as if she was searching for the right description. 'Like…there's something missing, y'know?'

A loud scrape caused their eyes to dart around the room until they discovered the source: it was just Jalen, pushing back his chair. Together, Damica and Dorian watched him journey along the curve of the table in pursuit of the windows.

'Do you think you could ever forgive her?' Dorian near-whispered.

Whatever her answer was, it would be for his ears only. Just like in their email friendship days.

Do you think you could forgive me too?

'I don't know,' Damica murmured. 'She held my hand and stuck by me through so much. Was that for her own gain sometimes? Sure. But she's my mom. There are days when I just want a hug from her. We went from talking, arguing—

whatever—pretty much every day to…nothing. I miss her, but I have to move on. And I can't be around her without the past looming over us, so…'

Remorse weighed down Dorian's heart. He imagined it must have been tough for Damica to read his passive aggressive jabs at her rebelliousness, when that same rebellion was the only freedom she'd ever known.

Jalen was now stationed by the glass, deliberately fogging up the surface with his breath and drawing smiley faces in the condensation. The animated curves were a direct contrast to the more subdued stretch of Damica's mouth.

'He really likes you.'

Dorian blinked. 'Hmm?'

He ached to run his fingers reassuringly along her forearm. But touch had never been a component of their relationship, and he didn't want to infringe on her personal space.

'Jalen,' she clarified at a barely audible volume. 'He hasn't shut up about you since you let him play on that bike a few days ago.'

A feeling of fulfilment flickered within Dorian, warming him like the beginnings of a sparking fire. 'Really?'

'Seriously—I'm not exaggerating.' Damica bit down on her lip, though the action was ineffective at dampening the quiet pride she glowed with. 'He's so energetic *all* the time… I miss being like that. Sometimes he's a handful, but he's a hundred percent worth it.'

'I understand...'

Only partially, though. The possibility that he might never have the fully-fledged honour of fatherhood pained him. But despite this sobering reality, Dorian was more concerned about the possible opportunity dangling before him, just within reach. The chance to repair the damaged relations between himself and Damica while spending time with her adorable nephew.

It would be a perfectly crafted distraction to help him forget about his failings as a man. An escape from how lonely he was in paradise. Three birds, one stone.

Dorian took aim, hoping that he wouldn't miss the shot.

'How long are you here for?' he enquired as casually as possible, so as not to raise Damica's suspicions.

To make use of his hands—which had grown clammy—he picked up his fork and resumed eating his meal.

'The next three weeks,' Damica confirmed, taking a sip of her water.

'Interestingly, so am I.'

Dorian was pleasantly surprised by how the timelines of their vacations were aligned, and momentarily disturbed by the jittery sensation breaking out across his stomach. Butterflies were the symptom of a nervousness that he hadn't experienced since mustering up the courage to ask out his boarding school crush. There was no place for that here, with his friend.

Did they still qualify as friends?

'I don't mind helping you look after him—if you ever need help, that is.'

There. The ball was firmly in her court now.

Damica tapped a manicured nail on the edge of her plate. The acrylic-ceramic combo produced a pinging effect that twanged at Dorian's valour.

'Are you sure?' she asked.

'Positive.'

How ironic, he thought, that he knew some of her deepest secrets and fears, but she was like a stranger to him in other ways.

'Well, okay… I don't see why not,' Damica agreed nonchalantly.

An uncomfortable silence followed, wherein Dorian fished for a response and emerged with nothing. Was this the part where he should crack a joke? About what, though? And if she didn't find him particularly funny, his efforts would be counterproductive…

Instead, Damica extended him a new invitation. 'Getting him to wind down at bedtime has been a…challenge. Maybe you could come over to our villa and help out?'

'Absolutely. I'll be there,' he said, with lifted spirits and a grin that spanned from ear to ear.

Clearly blown away by his eagerness, Damica smirked but kept her gaze lowered, dodging connection with his vision. Her reservations about him were mostly unshaken, it seemed. Nevertheless, a willingness to trust him was starting to peek through—which was better than being turned away altogether.

Dorian could work with this.

Noticing that Jalen had wandered back to the table, Dorian clapped his hands together mischievously, making a show of rubbing his palms together. 'Who wants dessert?'

'Me! Me! Me!'

Jalen jumped up and down, springing to heights that grasshoppers would envy.

Dorian couldn't help but chuckle at this—and at Damica's consequent warning about the dangers of too much sugar.

CHAPTER THREE

DAMICA FINISHED ANOTHER circuit around the living room, then determined the probability of the carpet being worn down by her restless feet. Craning her neck, she monitored where Jalen currently was—cocooned in a blanket at the intersection of the L-shaped cream-coloured sofa, teetering on the edge of sleep.

Her worries softened into a need to nurture and she changed course. Being mindful not to startle him, she eased down onto the leather couch and slowly put her arm around her nephew. After wiping away a string of drool and fixing his durag, she tucked him into the crook of her arm and listened to the steady rhythm of his breath.

Dorian is right, she realised.

Despite her scepticism about letting Jalen gorge on his pick of desserts, the large meal, new surroundings and general excitement had been more than enough to wear the infant out.

Damica gave props to the origins of her late-night fidgets, only to be lured into the whirlpool of overthinking for the umpteenth time.

Dorian was sexy now.

Objectively, there had never been a time when he had been 'bad' looking. But the pulse of desire ignited by his attentiveness and the soft, intimate hum of his voice over dinner had felt weird and…and *wrong*.

Probably just intrusive thoughts, she told herself. Her therapist said they were the junk mail and spam of the human mind.

When was the last time she'd had sex? Her libido was simply desperately mining for prospective partners to sleep with.

Right?

Right.

Haven't seen him in twenty years…

Meaningless attraction…

Nothing to see here…

Bound to end in resentment and tears…

A formal knocking at the door overpowered Damica's speculation and the forgotten cartoons airing on the TV.

Scrambling to her feet, she left Jalen to entertain himself with the television. On her traipse across the spacious living room, she willed herself not to pull down the hem of her shorts or fiddle with her bonnet.

Dorian was her friend. Just a…

She flung open the villa's door, ready to give

the Prince and his bodyguard a cool greeting. But her larynx temporarily fell short of speech upon seeing Dorian right there...looking exactly the same as he had a few hours ago. His stance—hands buried in his pockets and eyes appraising the neighbouring holiday homes—was casual.

All light had vacated the sky, transforming it into an ominous sheet of black that twinned with the water. The single glowing lantern that was fixed to the front of the villa illuminated all the dips and points in his striking side profile.

And, of course, Ravi was firmly posted behind him, glaring over at Damica to weed out any signs of threat.

She kept her words succinct. 'Hi.'

'Hello.' Dorian inclined his head and put his hands together briefly, as though in prayer. He kept his eyeline respectful—way above her chest and pert nipples, which she knew were visible through her tank top due to the chilly night air. 'How is he?'

'Practically asleep,' she reported with a playful undertone, moving aside so he could enter. 'You'd better get in here and work your magic.'

Ravi beat him to it, blocking the doorway and declaring soberly, 'I'll need to perform an optical sweep of the premises first, ma'am. Standard procedure.'

Damica's warmth vanished, leaving only a dry echo. 'Procedure...?'

It was a much-needed reality check.

Leaning around his bodyguard's immovable form, Dorian winced apologetically at Damica. 'Any chance we could skip this part, Ravi?'

'Standard procedure, Your Highness.'

Damica waved Ravi inside. 'It's fine.'

Naturally she was familiar with security detail routines, having often hired personal protection for herself in the past. Damica couldn't blame the guy for doing his job. Although his request had opened up a trapdoor to a basement of worries.

Attraction to Dorian came right alongside limited freedom. Additionally, true privacy would always be a finite resource. If being babysat by guards didn't bother them now, the constant surveillance from the media, royal correspondents and fans would smother them both later down the line. Frantic pleasure in exchange for a lifetime of restricted liberty wasn't a worthy trade-off.

'Don't forget to check under my bed,' she snarked softly. 'I definitely planted a bomb back there.'

Dorian's disapproving headshake did little to dim his growing amusement. Luckily, Ravi was out of earshot. 'Don't.'

'There's a crossbow and arrows too,' she added in jest, crossing her arms.

Random bursts of small talk kept them entertained during their wait for Ravi to give the all-clear on the house, and the oh-so-dangerous four-year-old still hypnotised by cartoons. Once he did so, Dorian wasted no time in following Damica's lead to the living room sofa.

Their visitors' entrance was akin to an energy boost for Jalen. Suddenly gone were his yawns and impending drowsiness, replaced with a new thirst for the night hours.

Damica tracked down the TV remote on the coffee table and punched the 'off' button with her thumb, whilst Dorian scooped up Jalen.

Like a duck taking to water, Dorian relocated to the child's bedroom and tucked him under the duvet. Damica trailed behind, leaning against the doorway and marvelling at how much of a natural Dorian was in a caregiving role. He'd even prepared a special bedtime story for Jalen— an epic tale about a young boy who ventured through a meadow of sheep. Clever.

During the strategically placed counting of sheep, Dorian's eyes sought her out and he requested her close company with a simple wave. The way he held her gaze made familiarity twang at her heartstrings.

Damica didn't know why this fatherly spirit came as any surprise. If Dorian was still the same man of his emails, then his reverence for children was still going strong.

She sidled over to the bed and eased down on the edge, careful not to disrupt Dorian's story-telling too much with the sudden deposit of her bodyweight on the mattress. With Jalen nestled between them, the adults waited patiently for sleep to come calling...

Damica and Dorian migrated to the back porch, creeping away from the adorable string of drool glistening along Jalen's chin and the soft snores zigzagging to the ceiling. They reclined on a pair of sun loungers whilst Ravi skulked in the shadows by the ajar door to Jalen's bedroom.

An enclosed swimming pool which resembled a Tetris piece was slotted perfectly between the villa and the all-encompassing ocean. In the darkness, the liquid might have been a walkway that spanned the parameters of for ever, venturing deep into the unknown and far beyond.

Her insignificance among the forces of nature should have squashed Damica's fears. Nonetheless, they flooded back into her psyche with the severity of a burst pipe. Taylor and Leroy were enjoying the resort's live music night, which would undoubtably involve lots of dancing and public displays of affection. Jalen was only a few yards away—he was safe...she wouldn't lose him for a second time. Better yet, she'd successfully got Jalen ready for bed tonight, which was very aunt-like and accomplished of her.

Damica could do this.

She could successfully be someone other than a celebrity.

She would.

She was in control.

Suddenly aware that she was almost lying next to Dorian in utter silence, Damica rushed to fill the auditory gap with noise.

At the same time as him.

'Do you—?'

'I was—'

The clash was instantly defused by the quiet harmony of their laughter. Alas, the peace was short-lived. In the darkness, Dorian's chuckle and the constant sigh of sea water was like an unanticipated caress. Panic lanced through Damica's nervous system.

'You go first.'

Oblivious to her inner turmoil, Dorian gestured at her. Those nimble fingers attached to those artistic palms only stroked the flames of—

Control.

She had lots of it.

Did she, though?

Dorian had swept in and not only put Jalen to bed, but also read him a bedtime story like some sort of childcare pro. Dorian knew exactly who he was outside of being a prince. Unlike hers,

Dorian's identity was clearly set in stone: prospective father and lover of the arts.

'Just so you know, I still haven't forgiven you. I probably never will,' Damica blurted out.

She knew that she'd come across as petty and childish. *Good.* That was her aim. It was low-hanging fruit, but destroying any progression between them meant she could predict the outcome.

'I'll apologise as many times as you need me to,' he vowed without hesitation.

Urgh.

Why did he have to be so noble?

'What I want…' Damica closed her eyes, intent on blocking Dorian out. Internally, she wished for the impossible—then blew out the flame representing her want for him with all her might. 'Is to go back in time…to before you ended everything.'

'Technically, it was you who finished the friendship between us.'

The crease bisecting Dorian's brow deepened with each passing second, as though a knife blade was probing at his brain. Remorse bloomed in Damica's conscience. Was it really worth it? Excavating old memories to distract her from her own sexual confusion?

'You weren't the only one who lost a friend that day. I kept waiting and waiting for you to reply to my last email and you never did.'

'It's not like I could have. My marriage didn't even last for seventy-two hours—the whole world was laughing at me,' Damica justified emptily.

Unsurprisingly, once discovering the nuptials between her and Zac, Damica's mother and the management team had forced the lovebirds to sign annulment papers.

'Wedding gate' had been the straw that broke the camel's back. Damica hadn't been able to re-sign herself to living a life where she couldn't even dictate her subpar love-life. Taking a plunge, she'd fired her mother and replaced her entire team. An era of daring artistic decisions and scandals had followed.

'Hey...'

Something smooth and cool captured her chin, keeping her anchored to the present. Dorian's thumb curled over the underside of her jaw, gently turning her face to meet his. Their eyes connected. She hated how her sadness was on full display for him. But in turn, his sorrows were reflected in the shine of his brown orbs.

'I'm not the whole world,' he said.

The fuel required for her to lash out was run-ning low, and a hollowness that she was well ac-quainted with crept in. It was the very same void that she'd desperately tried to fill with party-girl antics. And expensive alcohol. And controver-sial fashion choices. Anything that was bound to soil the 'good girl' image her mother and the Feir Channel had crafted.

Damica shifted further along her lounger, removing his touch. 'You're really gonna sit there and pretend that you wouldn't have said *I told you so*?'

Dorian emitted a long breath, which carried the weight of his repentance. 'I swear to you, I didn't mean half of those things I said.'

A loud and ugly scoff escaped Damica. 'You cared enough to type them out, though.'

'I wasn't thinking clearly!' Dorian insisted.

'You're being too loud…'

She suddenly became conscious of how far their noise might travel. The last thing she wanted was for Jalen to be woken by their arguing.

Dorian sat upright and turned his body towards her, planting his feet on the deck in the process. Disappointment contorted his features, sucking away all the joy and leaving a pinched husk in its wake.

Stress has aged him, she noted.

It had withered them both, her moral compass reprimanded her. And here she was, shoving away the only other person who could empathise with the pains of her upbringing.

Readjusting his volume to an appropriate level, Dorian took a new approach. 'Besides, you're hardly the only victim here. What you said about my relationship with my father—after I confided in you about him—was hurtful.'

'I...' He'd got her there. 'I'm sorry.'

'Even if I had attended your wedding,' Dorian went on, appearing to be trying to convince himself, 'security would have been a nightmare, and someone would have alerted the press...which would have created an even bigger mess.'

'In hindsight, it was never really about the wedding...'

She owned up to her past behaviour, confronting the ash and smoke left in the wake of her interpersonal wildfire. The dull ache of embarrassment cancelled out any of his magnetism.

'I don't think I even loved Zac. I just wanted to feel like I was in charge of something in my life at the time...and I wanted to see you.'

'Over the last—what? Nine years? Refusing to arrange that flight has been one of my biggest regrets,' said Dorian, making a revelation of his own.

'One of them...?' Damica zoomed in on that particular phrase. 'Good to know I made that shortlist,' she said gravely.

Dorian seemed to have developed a newfound fascination in the lifelines branching out over his open palms.

'First place goes to Daddy Dearest. Naturally,' he proclaimed wryly, although the accolade was tinged with a darkness that Damica was afraid to investigate. 'As much as I loathe him, we are cut from exactly the same cloth. His influence on me is inescapable. I should've fought...should still fight harder to be free of him.'

'You did, in your own way.'

Damica's selection of the past tense was carefully intentional. She wasn't qualified to speak definitively on the man he was today. Only the boy she'd grown up with.

A bittersweet tang came with this realisation, leaving her with no choice but to stomach it. She'd made her choice.

'You made a whole new identity for yourself through your art. Is that something you still do?'

'Yes.'

Dorian frowned. Damica damned herself for how eager she was to know the verdict of his quasi palm-reading. She couldn't even commit to the stupidity of her petty little grudge. Her aversion to discipline evidently ran deep.

'I recently submitted one of my paintings for an exhibition,' he went on. 'Under a pseudonym, so no one knew I was the artist. It was a nightmare trying to remove all traces of the oil paint from my skin...but worth it. The piece ultimately got to hang in Concarre's National Gallery.'

'Dorian...!'

Damica was momentarily rendered speechless at how casually he'd recalled a career-affirming achievement that other artists would likely commit murder to attain.

'That's…*sensational*. And so, *so* well deserved.'

As though it was yesterday, her mind was cast back to the email in which he'd first described his love of the medium of oil painting. The attached photos had been of pieces characterised by bold colour schemes and ambiguous brush strokes. It had been impossible for her to decipher whether he'd intended to depict a fox or the Eiffel Tower…

'My favourite part of it all is that I actually earned my place there—like everyone else.' Dorian's satisfaction was unmistakable. 'And my father wasn't in my ear, complaining about how painting is a "feminine interest". My talent opened that particular door for me—not *my title*.'

He enunciated each word as if it were scarlet and bloodied from the shameful history of war and colonialism that was inseparable from Western monarchies.

'You're lucky that your title gives you access to so many things,' Damica said, delivering a gentle, much-needed reminder of Dorian's privilege.

He might have been within touching distance, but the glaring difference in their claims to wealth and fame meant they were worlds apart sometimes. Right now, for instance. Their childhoods were a point of bonding, but Damica's working-class background, race and relationship with hard labour couldn't be erased or overlooked.

'Things most people would die for.'

Dorian ran a hand through his hair, tousling the composed waves. His head sank even lower—in shame—and he scratched at the back of his neck. 'I know…'

'Have you ever thought about giving up being a royal?'

She dug a fraction deeper, unsure of whether she would uncover a rock-solid royalist, firm in his ways, or a man who was malleable to differing political outcomes.

'You could escape from your dad and everything that way.'

'I've thought about it. Many times.'

He glanced over his shoulder, chancing a look in Ravi's direction, as though he fully expected to be arrested for treason. Just entertaining the idea of forfeiting his title was akin to a serious crime.

Ravi was unmoved.

Despite it being Dorian's political livelihood lying on the other side of her question, it was Damica's heartbeat that spiked and dipped. His answer would uncloak so much. About his morals. About the type of man he was. About how she would classify him moving forward.

Upon hearing him say, 'I doubt I would ever step away', she felt her buoyancy deflate.

She remained silent, out of fear that she would give away just how invested she had been in his reply. This was just a conversation between the two of them. Yet she felt as if she'd been thrust into a time machine, doomed to relive exactly the same crushing sensation she'd suffered when first reading that size twelve Segoe-font-typed email confirming that Dorian's duty and chains of obligation would always outrank her.

She'd be stupid to think otherwise.

Duh. Water is wet.

'On the surface, it seems like such an easy choice. Just leave. Simple.'

Dorian's justification was an unforeseen resuscitation.

'But in actuality I'm choosing between a gilded cage or being hunted down like an animal for the rest of my life. The devil you know is marginally better than the one you don't. I've been primed for one lifestyle only.' He appeared to be convincing himself, as well as convincing her. 'I won't survive in any other environment. See?' He clicked his tongue. 'Just like him.'

King Constantine VIII of Concarre was the image of tradition, and it was no secret that his son, as heir apparent, would follow in his footsteps. Ascension to the throne and reigning over his nation was Dorian's birthright.

Their physical similarity was certainly a popular subject amongst devout fans of the Sotiropoulos family, with side-by-side comparisons of Dorian and the young Constantine going viral every other week.

Nevertheless, where the King was a staunch champion of Concarre's ancestry and imperial legacy, Dorian represented the face of a nation with a liberal future. Or at least journalists seemed to think so. They consistently ran pop culture commentary pieces with headlines such as: *Monarchy, but Make It Woke: What Royals All Over the World Can Learn From Prince Dorian of Concarre.*

And it didn't hurt that he was a thirty-something male specimen who was easy on the eye.

Fourteen Reasons Why We're Totally Crushing on Prince Dorian this Valentine's Day!

Damica was inclined to remind Dorian that although he shared familial roots with Constantine, he was budding into being his father's polar opposite. The fruits of these efforts, the Concarri Youth Arts Foundation—or CYAF, as Dorian had commonly referred to it in his emails—was a fitting example to cite. After a long battle with his father, Dorian's foundation had taken down all the statues memorialising colonisers and replaced them with artworks by up-and-coming sculptors of Afro-Concarri descent.

Now that she was aware of Dorian's media

sleuthing in regard to her, making her own internet spying known to him was no longer such a humiliating prospect. The symmetry of their actions showed that a level of care still remained, even though they'd been on bad terms for so long. It was as if a part of him had always been with her, in spite of the self-righteous, self-deprecating art enthusiast and poetry-reader vacancy he'd left behind after their separation.

She would be a fool to divorce herself from such a kindred spirit.

Their past had a beginning, middle and end—a predictable outline that most stories abided by. They would never be teenagers again. Presently, they were easing into their thirties: a new decade of life and the opportunity to start anew was available.

Sleeping with him would cheapen their connection and expose her to a grey area, Damica rationalised. Strictly platonic friendships were more fun anyway. Solid. Dependable. And above all, she'd be guaranteed a commanding role at the steering wheel for the entire voyage of their relationship.

'It's never too late to control your narrative,' she told him. 'All the charity work you're doing speaks for itself anyway, but…'

She lowered her emotional guard and surrendered all weapons, communicating with him the way that had always worked best. Her therapist had surmised that Damica's ability to joke about things was a coping mechanism developed during her childhood, in order to deal with the trauma of growing up under the intense scrutiny of the world's stage. The therapist was highly educated and likely correct.

Notwithstanding that, for Damica and Dorian, cracking jokes had always been their version of a digitally transferred hug.

'Fan fiction's always an option,' she went on.

'You…cannot be serious,' Dorian deadpanned.

His fading frown lines and the restored twinkle in his eye were a giveaway that his spirits were rising. And it was Damica who was driving this particular forklift and lifting them.

'As serious as a heart attack…'

Rotating at the waist, Damica swung her legs off the edge of the reclining chair. Her knees lightly bumped against his. However, she centred her attention on sliding her feet into her flip-flops. Not on how the innocent brush of their skin made heat flood her flesh. His rearranging of his thighs so that they bracketed both of hers *didn't* make her bones sigh. At all.

She pressed her legs together, double-checking they were firmly closed. 'Keep it simple. You versus your father. Wrestling AU.'

'And AU means…?' He leaned in slightly, signifying his interest.

Damica dug her nails into the cushion of her

seat, anchoring her line of thinking. 'Another universe.'

As if he was genuinely tickled by the idea of him and his father reimagined as theatrical fighters, circling each other in a squared ring, a ridiculous chuckle erupted from the pit of Dorian's stomach.

And together they leapt into a rabbit hole swarming with tropes, terminology and internet memes...

It wasn't until her entire body was jostled, and shards of light tapped impatiently at her closed eyelids, that Damica realised that she'd fallen asleep whilst chatting with Dorian. What had started as minutes had extended into hours. The moon had since long departed, and the sun had embarked on its climb to the sky's peak.

A secure pair of arms was carrying her somewhere, bride-style... *Inside*, she barely managed to deduce. In a far-off place, two men were conversing in rapid Concarri. The pillow beneath her ear wasn't a regular one, but something like a wall that strained and vibrated. The slow, repetitive tempo of a heartbeat played in her ear like a private lullaby. A chest?

Mustering up every scrap of energy, Damica opened her eyes a smidgen. Through those slits of blurry vision she detected Dorian, right above her. His hair, messy. His lower jaw moving in sync with one of the voices. It must have been him who was cradling her so protectively.

Dorian's smell—an oud and bergamot fragrance—intoxicated her senses and lured her deeper into a slumberous oasis. Warm, earthy, fresh, sweet…

Damica surrendered once again to unconsciousness.

Between falling asleep at her computer and waking up to keyboard impressions marking her cheek, and this, there was no competition.

She nestled deeper into Dorian's warmth, welcoming dreams and nightmares and whatever else awaited her with open arms.

Age Fifteen

From: mrdoryfish7@inbox.com
To: damidiamondzzz@inbox.com
Subject: Hmm…

Dear Damica
Heyyyyy! I love you. I love you so much!
    Everyone always leaves.
    My mother left me, but you stay.
    I keep waiting for you to send emails…
    And I keep replying…respondink…and I just don't understand…

From: damidiamondzzz@inbox.com
To: mrdoryfish7@inbox.com
Re: Hmm...

Hey Dorian,
Are you DRUNK?
  LOL!
  What is going on here?
  XD
  Dami

From: mrdoryfish7@inbox.com
To: damidiamondzzz@inbox.com
Re: Hmm...

Dami,
My deepest, deepest apologies for my last email.
You must have been so confused. Please don't
take anything I typed seriously. I can barely understand it myself.
  Yes... I was drinking.
  One of the day students here at my school
managed to smuggle in a few bottles of vodka.
The toilets are one of the few places we have
any privacy, so someone stood watch at the door
there. The rest of us passed the bottle round
until it was empty.
  Fun in the moment, but not in the morning.
My head feels like it's being pounded. The worst
part? I have to hide the hangover, because if the

nurse finds out, everyone involved will get into trouble.

My bodyguard, Ravi, already knows, but he promised not to tell any of the teachers.

So, I'm safe! For now.

How are you doing? Tell me what life on tour is like.

From,
Dorian

From: damidiamondzzz@inbox.com
To: mrdoryfish7@inbox.com
Subject: Hmm... Part Two

I've heard of drunk texting before, but drunk emailing must be a new one.

LMFAO!

Very princely of you.

Life here isn't as exciting as you would think. We're currently in London, and I'm dying to go sightseeing, but all the shows and travelling make me really tired, and then I have to fit in the hours with my tutor, so I've mainly been sleeping and watching TV shows at hotels.

NEVER *Dani DoRight* or anything on the Feir Channel, though. I get enough of that already.

It's...hard. But performing is always fun.

Sometimes I wish I could sing my own stuff, but literally anything is better than school. I never miss it. Back when I still went, the other kids treated me like I was contagious because of my vitiligo. Now people stare and I give them a reason to, whilst doing something I actually enjoy

:)

Good luck on your mission of not getting caught! One time, my cousins let me drink with them and Mom caught us. She was not happy, but she's only happy with me when I'm working, so...

From,
Dami

From: mrdoryfish7@inbox.com
To: damidiamondzzz@inbox.com
Re: Hmm... Part Two

Okay, so apparently alcohol makes your breath smell!?

Mission failed.

I got called to the headmaster's office. I took all the blame, and now I have to spend my extracurricular hours volunteering at the school library.

It's not as boring as I thought it would be. And my friend Dario is here keeping me company because he is also in trouble. He says hi by the way!

:D

If you ever want someone else to read your songs and give a different perspective, send them my way. I started reading the work of Nizar

Qabbani, and I'm learning that poetry can actually be interesting and cool. Songwriting and poetry are basically the same thing, right?

I need as many distractions as possible right now. Someone must have told the press about my drinking...and the headlines are not on my side. Neither are the people of my country. I made the mistake of reading a comments section or ten. Weirdly, Father sent me a letter saying how 'pleasantly surprised' he was by my behaviour, and how he hoped it 'put some hair' on my chest.

How is that now almost everyone hates me, he decides to be proud of me?

From: damidiamondzzz@inbox.com
To: mrdoryfish7@inbox.com
Re: Hmm... Part Two

Dear Dorian

I went through something similar, but in reverse, so I feel you. I've always known who my dad is. He and Mom broke up after my little sister was born, and he chose not to be in our lives. He got back in touch after *Dani DoRight* got big, though...

Obviously, I didn't want to speak with him—none of us did. Next thing I knew, he was on all the big talk shows talking about how spoilt I was and saying that I'd forgotten my roots.

It was like he was suddenly everywhere, and everyone had something to say about the way I was treating him. But Mom was by my side the whole time...which was confusing, but not confusing.

For as long as i can remember it's only been the three of us. Mom and Taylor don't say it, but it's obvious that it's my job to earn money for all of us. I like acting and everything...the pressure is a lot to deal with, though. I feel like i can never quit because then Mom will be mad at me. However, she gets mad at me a lot these days. Disappointed might be better...

I never forget what our life was like before, when she would stress over bills and stuff. That's why smoking is good, I think. Once i got over the chicken noodle smell, it was relaxing and fun. Just for a while I can forget about everything, chill and be normal.

So, yeah, I get what you're going through.

I'm not gonna tell you to just keep your head up, because I hate that phrase, and you might too.

From,
Dami

PS Thanks for offering to take a look at my songs. I've attached a few. Lemme know what you think! Not sure if it compares to the work of a poet.

CHAPTER FOUR

'AND THEY'RE OFF!'

Dorian gave a live commentary on the flurry of children dashing across the beach in pursuit of the sea. The mini stampede conjured up a collective cloud of sand grains with its demanding feet. Dorian might as well have been a grand prix spectator, viewing a party of racing cars zooming around the grid—after all, each and every kid was a personalised machine, fuelled by energy and an eagerness to win.

Amongst them, in the lead, was Jalen. Dorian had pulled a few strings to get him a place in Club Enfant—a group within the resort that organised fun activities for any children currently visiting. By 'strings', he meant royal influence. Unsurprisingly, the overworked summer staff had been more than happy to accommodate a last-minute enrolment on behalf of Concarre's prince.

Dorian supposed he was being a hypocrite, having complained about the crippling woes of being born into elite power and privilege last night to Damica. Although providing some fun for Jalen felt like a worthy cause. Being able to contribute to the care of a young child was a reward. Life itself was a gift. And if Dorian didn't have the full capability of procreating, he wanted to be able to pour his love into any child that was in his presence.

'I'm blue and I'm deep…you can find me by the sea.' Damica recited the first clue in the Club Enfant treasure hunt, the reason for the racing competition. 'Let's go.'

Dorian hitched the handle of his parasol higher, taking the portable shelter and shade with him as he followed the kids. They'd been informed by the club staff that parents, guardians and carers were welcome to participate in all activities. Not wanting to cramp Jalen's style in front of his new friends, they'd opted for inconspicuous supervision at a distance, with none other than Ravi bringing up the rear.

Dorian's sandalled feet sank into the uneven shore, making the journey uneven and more laborious than he'd expected. Granular gold sand unforgivingly invaded whatever and whichever gaps presented themselves—namely the gaps between his toes. He winced slightly at the piercing heat of the sunbaked sand on the sensitive grooves of his skin.

Beside him, Damica's arm accidentally bumped

into his own. His heightened senses interpreted the innocent touch as a searing stroke. The tumble of her braids around her shoulders attracted his attention to their bareness. His piqued vision latched on to the way the thin strap of her blush-pink dress was teetering on the very edge, threatening to slide down her upper arm…

This was highly inappropriate.

Dorian cleared his throat suddenly. Loudly. Mainly to catch at his wandering concentration. Far, far away at a signpost planted at the sea's edge, the children had congregated, already working on solving the next clue.

'Very straightforward riddle,' he said. 'A bit too easy. I know they're young, but…'

What was he even saying?

'The poet aficionado has spoken,' Damica teased him—which, in all honesty, only fanned the flames of his nerves.

At the same time, he couldn't help flirting with fire. Once would hardly maim him. After all, romance was incredibly fleeting. Sexual urges to a higher degree.

But friendship was the best setting for them. The foundation was firm, built to last, and it had evidently survived the last storm they'd weathered. He'd missed their joint talent for conversing so easily about a deep, personal topic in one breath, and something silly and inconsequential in the next.

Dorian feigned modesty. 'You're too kind…'

'In my opinion, *"replying…respondink"* is your best work by far,' Damica quipped, calling back the drunken message that had once been a running joke between them. 'Your magnus opus.'

He sent her a wink. 'I'm planning to publish it soon. You won't be disappointed.'

They picked their way across the scorching sand until they reached the soothing tide of the water. Along the way, they made sure to stick within the cooled cocoon of the parasol's shade to move as one.

Damica's vitiligo meant she was susceptible to sunburn, so Dorian took the responsibility of providing her safety very seriously. Keeping the umbrella poised over her head, he slipped off his shoes and hooked them onto the fingers of his free hand along with the opaque water bottle filled with the protein shake recommended by his nutritionist. Not necessarily his preferred drink of choice.

After taking a second to appreciate the frothy white waves rolling over their bare feet, and the azure expanse up above, Damica flipped over the laminated card attached to the post.

'I'm very tall and have green leaves,' she read aloud. 'You can see me where there's lots of…'

'Trees.' Dorian solved the clue effortlessly.

He gestured at the island, which was laden

with evergreen and shrubbery, situated within the ocean's stretch. The objects suspended from his fingers knocked together but thankfully nothing fell.

The speedboat zapping across the water was critical proof that he was correct about the next location. Inside the vessel, the youngsters and the club leaders—all wearing lifejackets—faded into obscure orange blobs. Their endless chatter blended in with the retreating sound of the engine.

Going... Going... Gone.

'We can get a boat from the marina,' Damica advised.

No map needed, they plodded along the wet shoreline, liquid sloshing around their ankles as they inched further along the resort's coastline towards where a group of boats, yachts and jet skis were roped in the harbour. The watercraft bobbed as if in anticipation. The sporadic movement caused sunlight to blink harshly off their sleek surfaces, inviting Damica and Dorian to come forth.

Dorian's exhilaration swelled to new proportions. He marvelled at how a simple daytime children's treasure hunt could make him feel like an adventurer depending on the North Star.

'This is fun.'

'Very.'

Her eyes snagged his, and her tone mirrored

his enthusiasm. The casual swing of her arms and the dangle of her flip-flops fed into their shared pleasure.

'I thought you'd be more competitive,' he said.

Curiosity sparked in him upon the realisation that, despite knowing her from the ages of thirteen to twenty-four, there was a whole chunk of Damica-related knowledge missing from his personal records. Dorian was well versed in the ins and outs of the mistrust she felt towards her father, and the extensive lore of her songwriting. However, when it came to other matters…like whether she preferred to drink coffee or tea in the mornings…he was coming up blank.

The nine-year deficit in their relationship exposed his familiarity with the girl of the past, not the woman at his side now. No amount of internet research could compensate for that.

Did she still dream of matching mother and baby outfits?

'I can be competitive…' She made a *so-so* motion with her hand. 'When a situation requires me to be.'

Dorian found that he was surprisingly desperate to unlock this side of her. To unwrap all the possible dimensions of her personality so he could appease the gluttonous monster formed of his inquisitiveness. His want was so intense it sucker-punched his gut, triggering nausea.

Wrong. Everything about this was wrong.

Why was he so intent on soiling the one thing that was going right?

Grappling with logic, he sought out the nearest sign that pointed to how incompatible he was with Damica on a romantic level.

'Ravi?' He addressed his bodyguard, who was a breath away behind them on a dry stretch of the sand. Fully clothed, he was a pillar of black material and muscle. The only signifier that the heat was getting to him was the folded handkerchief he was dabbing his damp forehead with. 'You can take your shoes and jacket off, if you wish. Enjoy the weather with us.'

'I'm fine, Your Highness. Thank you, though.'

Ravi's conviction was flimsy, at best, but Dorian knew better than to prod.

Besides, his turn to sweat arrived when they neared the marina. A guest transportation system of sorts was in effect, whereby a rotation of speedboats manned by resort staff travelled to and from the mainland and the island. They'd already missed the Club Enfant's ride, and if the queue forming on the dock was anything to go by they would have to wait a while for the next available speedboat.

Sensing Damica growing angsty at the prospect of Jalen being away from her view for that long, Dorian fished for a solution.

Thinking quickly, he flagged down the harbourmaster and sweet-talked him into renting them a rowing boat. That was the easy part. The real challenge was getting Ravi to hand over the proverbial reins.

Dorian couldn't blame the bodyguard for taking his role so seriously. He could only imagine the severity of punishment awaiting Ravi if the future sovereign of Concarre was to be put in harm's way under his supervision. Nonetheless, he failed to see the fun in having to bargain for his freedom on his own holiday.

Their negotiation process was one he was all too familiar with. Varying terms would be shot between them like bullets from the guns at a cowboy shoot-out.

Dorian cheerily proceeded to where the sailboat was waiting for them. The trick was to open discussions by demanding way more than he knew he would receive.

'I'll row us there and back,' he said.

'That won't be possible, Your Highness.'

Ravi overtook him, plonking down onto the craft. Then a rarity occurred. He landed heavily amongst the wooden oars, and his thick arms flapped in the air to help him regain his balance. The moment vanished just as quickly as it transpired. Once Ravi's equilibrium was restored, he lifted his elbow, offering himself as a handrail to assist Dorian in stepping down onto the boat.

In mutiny, the Prince backed away into the

shade cast by Damica's parasol. 'I'll just row there, then.'

'Don't forget to put your lifejacket on.'

'Only if you let me row us there. Take it or leave it.'

'I have no issues with us staying here on the mainland, Your Highness.'

'Whoa… We can't *not* go!'

Damica's alarm powered the broadness of Dorian's smirk. Little did she know he had Ravi exactly where he wanted him.

'I can row us there. Lifejacket on. And tomorrow we'll have a lazy day at the pool, so I'll be easy to watch.'

Ravi was betrayed by the twitch of one of his eyelids and the pesky bead of sweat sliding down the side of his face to hang off his chin. The hot weather was taking its toll on him.

Dorian banked on the fact that Ravi was a man unmoved by favours or bribes. Practicality was the only way to win him over. The guarantee of an easy workload tomorrow, especially in a climate such as this, would be irresistible.

'We…have a deal, Your Highness.'

As predicted, Ravi caved.

Dorian pumped a victorious fist. The exaggerated roll of Damica's eyes did little to suppress her peals of laughter.

Accepting the lifejacket she shoved in his direction, Dorian put on the inflated nylon garment with the pride of a superhero.

'We'll definitely be taking a speedboat back to the mainland,' Ravi ordered sullenly.

Dorian saluted him. 'Sir, yes, sir.'

Ignoring the assistance of his bodyguard's arm, he descended from the dock and into the boat independently. The insinuation that he was made of glass, especially in front of Damica, bothered Dorian more than it should have. A tiny worry pricked at his ego, about how she might side with his father in his assessment of Dorian as weak and wimpish.

Under his feet, the boat rocked. However, he was so expectant of the jolt that it simply spurred him on.

Elaborately, he presented a hand upward to Damica. 'My lady...'

His outward humour countered the onslaught of inner shyness triggered by her close analysis of his palm. Her touch hovered over his, as though she feared she was about to come into contact with an unverified substance. The feather-light graze of her smooth, soft skin sent a pleasant heat up Dorian's forearm and bicep.

'Why, thank you, kind sir.' Damica's lips twisted into a sheepish smile, and she adopted a British accent to play along with his façade of chivalry. Only for Dorian it wasn't pretence.

She gracefully pressed her hand into his, allowing him to help her on to their new mode of transportation. His fingers clasped hers dutifully, his thumb closing around her knuckles like the snug fit of an envelope seal.

See—he *was* strong.

To his disappointment, an awkward shuffle around Ravi forced him to release Damica.

Lowering herself onto the bench stationed across from Dorian, she tittered. 'I can't believe how seriously you're taking this.'

'Because I've never done this before.'

Dorian gingerly took the glossy wooden oars awaiting him from their thick collars. His very first attempt at rowing gave the phrase 'a fish out of water' new meaning. Nonetheless, he simply tried again.

'I'm like a kid in a candy shop!'

His chuckles were intertwined with the audible strands of Damica's happiness, creating an inseparable structure.

As soon as he got the hang of the rhythm, he indicated for Ravi, who was situated in the hull, to untie the rope mooring the boat to the mainland marina. More confident in his ability this time, Dorian pushed and pulled at the oars. Their movement soon synced with the water's, and the boat drifted further out to sea.

Under the blaze of the sun, and in the throes of such heavy exercise, Dorian felt a thin layer of perspiration break out over him. Beneath his lifejacket, his shirt clung to his chest. He made sure to keep his breathing measured and consistent.

Damica's quietness and her steady examination of his flexing biceps threatened to derail the systemic to-and-fro of his movements. Yet he was enjoying being subjected to what he sorely hoped was her admiration.

The periodic splashing, the creak of the wooden oars and Dorian's breathing pattern were the only components bridging their noiselessness. His rowing persisted—with more vigour. Up and down. In and out. Coming and going. Did he appear confident and capable and manly, from her viewpoint? Because that was how he felt.

From under the heavy shadow of her parasol, Damica's dark eyes bored into him. He matched their glowing intensity, well aware that he was infringing on dangerous territory. If this was a siren's call, then he wasn't a poor, unsuspecting sailor, but rather a willing sacrifice.

The point of her tongue emerged from her mouth to wet her soft, parted lips…

And then the spell was broken as something flickered across Dorian's visual field.

A blink later, and Damica was one-handedly rummaging around the collection of objects scattered over her lap. Dorian put down the oars, using the opportunity to regain his strength and identify the source of the intervention: a pesky lock of hair had fallen over his face.

By the time he'd tucked it behind his ear and dried his sweaty hands on his shorts Damica was waving his drink bottle at him. Her downcast eyes and her preoccupation with the container's spectacularly uninteresting design exhibited how flustered she was. Apparently, he wasn't the only one who'd got a little carried away.

'Here. You should take a break.'

The tightness reigning over his muscles switched from being provocative to something to be feared. Stiffly, he took the bottle from her and unscrewed the lid. The glare of the stain-less-steel lining made him tense up even more, as though the light attracted even more attention to the bottle's contents. Meanwhile, his activity meant the boat was gradually being ushered off-course by the jumping waves.

'Everything all right, Your Highness?'

Ravi put forward the hushed query, from his corner of the vessel.

'I'm fine.'

The swig Dorian took was mostly for show. His tastebuds barely registered the smooth blend of raspberries, banana, kale and various other in-gredients. Their ingestion solidified in his stom-ach like a stone of shame. Shoving the resealed bottle on the floor somewhere behind him, he carried on rowing, this time closing his eyes.

The poisoned chalice might be out of his sight, but out of mind it was not.

A sturdy fitness regime and diet plan were meant to be a practical long-term solution to improving his reproductive health. But no matter how much this domestic illusion he was in with Damica felt like a quick fix, it wasn't.

They could never be.

Plus, who was he to assume that Damica would even want to commit to him romantically? The fact that his little swimmers couldn't swim properly was intriguing at best and devastatingly emasculating at worst.

He could take being a plaything for the Concarri national press and media. And as much as he hated it he'd learnt to tolerate his father's countless jibes at his artistic endeavours. But his friendship with Damica had always been his safe space. Nothing could ruin that for him. Not the faintest whiff of a dalliance. Definitely not a serious relationship. And certainly not her finding out about his infertility.

It wasn't until he brought the boat to a safe stop at the island marina that Dorian felt he could exhale properly. After the docking process, he fulfilled his duty of helping Damica alight from the watercraft, and used the little composure he had left to stretch out his sore muscles.

The three of them approached the jungle, basking in the coolness provided by the network of trees. Light filtered in through the intricate lattice of branches and leaves overhead, which gave everything a green hue. Dorian was so overpowered by his own awe that he didn't immediately realise Damica had fallen a step behind.

'Everything okay?'

He paused to seek her out, meaning Ravi halted too. A chain reaction was now in effect.

'I just need a minute,' she told him, pressing the button to close her parasol. Slinging the collapsed canopy over her shoulder as if it was a bindle stick, she spun around. 'I love it here.'

The circular billow of her skirt, the languid purr and high praise for their new environment made him think of a Channel Feir princess. Given her history with the Feir conglomerate, Dorian knew she would heavily oppose any association with them. But her delight was so pure and magical. There was no other way to describe it.

'I can tell,' he remarked fondly. 'Do you want me to get a picture of you?'

'I forgot to grab my phone on the way out this morning.'

'I think I have mine…'

Dorian patted the front pockets of his shorts. Then the back. Nothing. Uh-oh. Amidst the rush to shed his lifejacket, he hadn't bothered to check whether he had all his belongings. Speaking of which, where was his bottle…?

Damica's extended arm looked all the more tempting when he noticed that she was in possession of his drinking container. Her blush-pink manicured nails were distinct against the royal blue. A sick reminder of the two worlds he wished to keep segregated at all costs.

Panic caused him to walk towards her more quickly than he would have liked. Oblivious to the cause of his anxiety, Damica danced away from his lurch.

'Damica…' He chastised her gently, walking over to her new spot.

'Yes?' She played dumb, side-stepped out of his range.

This was an immature game she was playing, and yet he entertained it. If her aim was to stress him out, she was winning.

Dorian froze…then struck when she least expected it. 'Give it—'

'Need something?'

She jumped away in the nick of time. Dorian's fingertips swept past her swishing braids.

'Give it back!' He tried again, but his effort was futile.

Impassive as ever, Ravi trod towards Dorian to keep him within close range. The domino effect wasn't lost on Damica. A mischievous glint dawned in her eyes before she took off down the nearest trail.

'Damica…come on! Seriously?'

Without a second thought, Dorian sprinted after her. As might have been expected, his hurried footfall was echoed by the uniform thump of Ravi's boots. Embarrassingly, his bodyguard's stamina made Dorian's panting seem all the more loud.

Damica was a faster runner than Dorian had presumed. The joke was on him for underestimating her. She led them down a turn here… around a corner there. She even had the audacity to giggle, which made Dorian's blood boil with the fierce flavour of competition.

He *would* catch her.

Pushing through the unheavenly burn of his quads and his calves, Dorian galloped over a spindly tree root obtruding onto the footpath. Woefully, Ravi didn't see the same obstacle quickly enough. An angry string of curse words punched at the air, followed by a calamitous smack and a skid.

'Your Highness—Dorian—stop!'

A crossroads of decisions presented itself.

Follow the rules or break the rules.

Obey the commands of his bodyguard and stay under his scrutiny like a good little boy.

Or keep on with Damica's bizarrely fun game of tag.

Deeper and deeper into the web of paths and thick forestation Dorian went, keeping the swoosh of Damica's skirt and the flashes of her bare thighs within his sight. Ravi's shouts were replaced by the bird calls reverberating from the treetops.

Dorian mimicked their sounds, succumbing to a juvenile nature he'd never been allowed to fully acquaint himself with. It, tag, hide-and-seek—whatever the name of this game was—was highly thrilling. A brief, much-needed deflection from his worries over his father's appraisal of his manhood and whether he would ever be fertile enough to become a father the good old-fashioned way.

All that mattered was that he was with Damica, fooling around.

She vanished around yet another bend. Taking a risk, Dorian chose to jog down a path that ran parallel to her route. Through the greenery, he spied her slowing to a stop, mistakenly assuming she was safe.

'Give up!' he yelled menacingly, between gulps of oxygen,

'Never!'

Caught by surprise, Damica started up again, traipsing onward—only to reach a dead end. She winced, and then hotfooted it back down the path.

However, Dorian was speedier. He retreated

to the place where the two pathways diverged.
'Aha!'

'No!' she whined at her defeat.

'Oh, yes…'

He must've looked like a madman, spreading
his arms wide and jigging on each foot in his
attempts to block all possibility of her escape.
A far cry from the controlled Prince who could
never afford to put so much as a foot wrong.
And if Damica was repulsed, she was expertly
hiding all traces of disgust behind that same un-
readable, beautiful expression she'd worn on the
boat ride over.

She pulled back. Dorian prowled towards
her, this time unhindered by the way his hair
was flopping over his eyes. A hunter's instinct
eclipsed his rationale for a nanosecond. He could
go in for the kill right now and snag her plush
lower lip between his teeth.

Not that he ever would.

But it was a positively electrifying prospect,
he admitted to himself. In this place where there
were no witnesses…

In an instant, Dorian was back in reality and
mindful of the rattling of liquid and a faint prodding at his sternum. His bottle. Half full of a
possible improvement to improving his sperm's
health. Yes. The object of this wild goose chase.
Damica was yielding the prized object, pressing

the plastic cylinder to his breastbone with an audaciously innocent smile.

Dorian snatched it back, chest still heaving from the unforeseen workout. The ease flooding his nervous system overrode any anger.

'What are you playing at?'

'It worked.' She turned away to inspect the seat of a nearby bench, then dusted off the back of her dress. Sinking down, she noted, 'You look a lot more relaxed without a bodyguard attached to your every move.'

'So…you're telling me…this was part of a… grand plan to…?'

Suddenly Dorian's tunnel vision vanished, uncloaking the area where they stood and revealing a clearing of sorts, right in the heart of the labyrinthine jungle. The space looked boundless—even more so because he knew he was free to scale a tree without Ravi interrogating all the wildlife beforehand.

'To break you out of your castle and show you the world outside? Yes.'

Damica crossed one leg over the other, wriggling her dangling foot. The rotation of her ankle enticed his view to climb higher, to her shin and beyond. Instead, he pivoted his focus to his own feet which, like Damica's were caked in a mix of sand, dirt, dust and sweat.

Dorian wiped a hand across his jaw to get rid

of the gathered moisture and the silly grin. 'Ravi's going to be furious.'

'Enraged!'

'Seething.' His mirth only tripled.

'We both know how the saying goes…' Damica patted the empty spot next to her on the bench. 'Ask for forgiveness. Not permission.'

Dorian trudged over to the wooden seat, wincing at how sore his leg muscles were. Collapsing onto the seat, he told her facetiously. 'There will be serious ramifications for the Maldivian government if anything happens to me on their soil…'

'Which it won't. I'm a pro at this,' she bragged, whilst giving his arm a reassuring squeeze.

He rested his eyes. His muted senses made the smell of Damica's signature perfume even stronger.

'I figured.'

'And I was lying before. I did bring my phone.'

Dorian's right eyelid opened a smidgen, so he could see her take her touchscreen device out of her drawstring shoulder bag.

'We can contact Ravi to tell him where we are.'

'He's going to be so ma-a-ad,' Dorian sing-songed, causing them to fall into another fit of giggles.

'Yeah…the fallout is usually the worst part.

But the brief moments of peace always make it worth it.'

She closed her bag and copied his manner of sitting, leaning on the support provided by the bench's backrest and tilting her neck back slightly.

'Like when we first met.'

Dorian kept on sneaking the occasional sideways peek in her direction. He couldn't have agreed more. Defiance with Damica was a sweet escape from the constraints he'd known his whole life and the string of anxieties bonded together by his royal obligation. The result of was…this. A quiet, insulated life, in which Dorian could cater to the whim of his inner child, whilst fulfilling his other wish of caring for a child of his own.

This was a perfect dream.

He wasn't ready to wake up just yet.

Dorian reflected on ways to preserve such a peaceful, precious moment, and Damica served as the perfect muse. Snapping a picture seemed instant and distasteful. And furthermore, the idea of breaking down her complexities into basic paint blobs of blue, red and yellow—the primary colours—felt almost insulting.

Not even his thinnest brush could reproduce her damp glow and the curled spring of her baby hairs. Plus, he hadn't packed any painting equipment for the trip. All he had was his trusted sketchbook and a tin of pencils ranging from HB to 4B. So, a drawing would have to do.

A gust of birdsong broke through nature's quiet and the utter serenity of Damica's upturned face. She squinted up at the rustling treetops and the jungle vine sprawled across the chunky bark like emerald scales.

'Asian Koel. Resident birds here,' Dorian said, educating her. 'Also known as *dhivehi koveli.*'

Damica expressed how impressed she was with a hum. 'Okay, Mr Discovery Channel… Does Sir David Attenborough have some serious competition now?'

'Not quite. I just read it in one of the resort brochures.'

It was during this amateur wildlife lesson that they noticed the next treasure hunt clue, nestled in the intersection of two tree trunks. And so on to the next location—the tennis courts—they went.

Dorian's newfound disobedient streak continued as he rowed himself and Damica back to the mainland to collect Jalen from the concierge desk. Once more like a kid in a candy store, he feasted on this bad behaviour at the ripe old age of thirty-three. Such delinquency was some compensation for all the childhood holidays he hadn't got to have. This was what he was owed.

He regretted ever asking for permission, and the begging for forgiveness from Ravi was all for show.

CHAPTER FIVE

'ARE YOU SURE this thing is safe?'

Damica was unable to hide her scepticism as she eyed the surf simulator set up in the middle of the beach. According to the Club Enfant timetable for Saturday morning, catching a few machine-generated waves was the perfect activity to commence the day.

'Says the woman who left the Met Gala mid-event on the back of a motorcycle!' Dorian guffawed. 'With no protective headgear.'

'That was my interpretation of that year's theme.'

'Fantasy and Fashion…?'

'Are motorcycles not the motor vehicle equivalent of dragons?' she asked, trying to legitimise the link. 'And there weren't any kids involved—back me up here, Ravi.'

Straight away, Damica felt remorseful about dragging the royal bodyguard into her light-hearted quarrel with Dorian. The only acknowledgement he gave was a rebuking glower, and his scornfulness notified them that their promise of a lackadaisical day by the pool and an uneventful remainder of the week wasn't an apology that was proportional to his tumble on the jungle island.

Damica and Dorian were inclined to agree, and so Ravi's silent treatment went largely unchallenged.

'We can investigate it ourselves,' Dorian declared, taking her hand and gently dragging her over to the aqua blue simulator. 'It's open to adults too, remember?'

Without thought, she laced her fingers through his as they made their way past where the instructors were helping the group of excitable kids into lifejackets and trying to talk them through the health and safety measures.

She could see that any distrustful parents and guardians were indeed welcome to have a turn on the simulator. Up close, Damica made note of the machine's diagonal angle, and how the jets lining the sides sent water cascading down the slope. The instructor in charge presented them with the mandatory lifejackets and some facts about the machine's design. Damica perceived most of it as unintelligible, but Dorian seemed engrossed by the ins and outs of its engineering.

After the impromptu Q&A session had drawn to a close, Dorian kicked off his flip-flops and helped Damica onto the simulator.

'Turn that frown upside down!' he said.

A glum Ravi stayed on the sidelines, dwarfing the simulator instructor, who was attempting to make small talk. Never would Damica have guessed that she'd find common ground with the bodyguard through cynicism.

There had been a pronounced change in Dorian since their defiant dash through the jungle. He was louder…and looser…and less concerned with upholding a respectable image. Secretly, she'd never been prouder of being a 'bad' influence. Their fight to exist as two normal human beings for an afternoon had been worth it. Just like all the other unruly outbursts that had dotted her adolescence.

Now, they crossed the slanted terrain of gushing water, shivering at the cold their bare feet were subjected to. Damica gingerly climbed onto the surfboard fixed to the floor—its surface was already slick.

The hold Dorian had on her hips vied with the snugness of her bikini bottoms. The press of his fingertips into her flesh seemed to correlate with the delicious heat blossoming at the pit of her stomach. But she hastily disregarded the sensations altogether, clinging to the stability of his shoulders instead.

'Are you okay?'

'I'm good!'

They shared a comforting smile until she was confident enough to stand on her own.

However, in the short time it took for Dorian to sprint over to the matching surfboard, a few meters away, she felt a yearning ache leak into her wits.

Was that his version of trying to cop a feel?

Should she be mad about his hypothetical fondle?

She *should* be, but…

Having clambered onto his own surfboard, Dorian gave her a shaky grin and a thumbs-up. 'Ready?'

With no forewarning, the board swivelled and jerked underneath her feet, robbing her of the chance to speak. The only sounds her larynx could produce were pathetic whimpers. Out of desperation, Damica bent her knees and thrust out trembling arms, desperately seeking to centre herself amid the chaos that had been introduced to her equilibrium.

The simulator was now in full force. Even the water settings had increased and had gone into a new mode, with liquid streaming down the blue flooring in hefty bursts.

To her left, Dorian's cackling was continuous—despite the fact that he was only mildly better than her at combating the onslaught of unpredictable movement below him.

Damica's jaw dropped. 'Seriously?'

Their circumstances hindered her ability to hurl any coherent accusation his way.

'Huh?' Dorian was goading her.

'You…*you*!'

'Yes?'

He was *laughing* at her.

She couldn't allow this disrespect to continue.

The dormant competitiveness that resided deep within her was harshly awoken. Tapping into her performer's instinct, she determined to treat her movements on the surfing simulator like a complex dance sequence. She looked ridiculous, sticking out her tongue, flapping her arms about and drawing erratic shapes with her waist, but gradually, she got the hang of things, distributing her body weight and balance to the necessary parts of her feet at any given time.

From her heels to the balls of her feet and back again, she met the frantic gyration and revolving of her surfboard, finally cracking the code. But in order to concentrate so intensely she'd decluttered her mind of all obstructive data, so she wouldn't get sidetracked—her apprehension about the simulator's safety included.

Just as she asserted her dominance over this realistic imitation of one of nature's most powerful elements, a blurred mass slipped, slid and then hurtled downward in her peripheral vision.

'Dorian!'

Damica was so terrified that the sequence of

Dorian's accident unfolded in muddled order. Her knees crashed down into the shallow pool of water and droplets flew everywhere—into her hair, eyes and open mouth. At lightning speed she was kneeling beside him, where he was sprawled out on the floor like a woozy starfish. At some point the simulator had stopped.

The pounding of her heart and a panicked rush of blood inhabited her eardrums. Her heart jackhammered against her ribcage. Her tongue was a useless organ, weighing down her mouth.

'Dorian…?'

'Your Highness?'

That was Ravi. He delicately elbowed her out of the way, so that he could check Dorian's wrists and neck—feeling the pulse points to see if he was still alive…conscious.

Oh, thank goodness—he was still breathing.

Unsure exactly what to do with her quaking hands, Damica tented them around her nose and mouth. Was she praying? She didn't classify herself as religious. But if there was the tiniest inkling of a chance that any higher power existed, she was reaching out and imploring that they save the man she loved from harm.

When she'd longed for freedom, she hadn't meant the removal of—

'Dorian…stay with me. How many fingers am I holding up?'

Ravi's gravelly rasp had been reduced to the

kind of frail whisper that nurses used on ailing patients. He was holding up three digits before Dorian's bleary eyes, conducting a further examination of the Prince's condition.

Dorian lay on his back. So still. So...serene. He was thoroughly drenched. The soles of his feet and his fingers were wrinkly and prune-like. His hair was plastered to his skull.

Although unlikely, she speculated over the possibility of those strands protecting him from concussion. The fibres of the lifejacket formed a bulky layer over his chest, so it was difficult to judge the inhale and exhale of his lungs by eye alone.

The Prince's fall had garnered the attention of the children, the Club Enfant staff and other parents and guardians. More and more people were flocking to the simulator entrance, peeping over the blue wall as though they were participating in a communal coffin-viewing.

Ravi barked at the instructor, demanding— with a few expletives tossed in—that they bring him a first aid kit and call for an ambulance.

Medical intervention meant this was serious. Serious enough that any injury Dorian had sustained would mean repercussions for the Maldivian government. Protests? Economic sanctions? War?

Suddenly Dorian's unmoving state was ruined by a faultless chuckle. The corners of his closed eyes creased, and the corners of his lips curled upward.

'I'm fine. Everybody can relax.'

Suspicious about the Prince's miraculous recovery, Ravi repeated his order for an ambulance.

But Dorian undulated his arms and legs in perfect unison, as if that was enough proof of his good health. The motion caused the water to ripple all around him.

'Not quite a snow angel, but close enough,' he said.

Damica sagged, her bottom connecting with the floor—which was a lot softer than she would have expected. Perfect for breaking falls and absorbing the energy of high-speed collisions. All at once her body's adrenaline supply was disconnected, plunging her into what should have been relief.

She didn't know whether she wanted to punch him…or kiss him.

Soon after the mishap, Dorian grudgingly agreed to hang out in among the picnic benches, out of action's way but within breathing distance of the surf simulator. Jalen had decided he was a young medical professional, and had provided him with a towel, so that he could dry himself off, and an ice cream to sweeten his stomach.

'Thank you, Dr Jalen,' said Dorian, playing along.

Sitting across from the small boy, he waited for Jalen to finish making his 'medicine'. Stirring runny ice cream with a plastic spoon clearly deserved alchemy-grade precision, and the adults respected his process.

Damica took a sideways glimpse at Dorian, who was invested in Jalen's pretence with the utmost sincerity. The towel hung around his neck like a scarf, the material the only barrier to his bare chest now that his lifejacket had been discarded. He absentmindedly pushed a hand through the damp mass of his hair and she seized the chance to appreciate his tanned face. Kind eyes. And his nose—which luckily wasn't broken!

The ebb and flow of her distress had lessened substantially now that it had been confirmed he was all in one piece. However, Damica had no choice but to reckon with the knowledge her dread had unmasked.

She...*loved*...him.

Fidgeting on her perch, she extended her neck and looked around the umbrella pole attached to the tabletop's centre and over Jalen's shoulder.

'The group's about to start surfing. You don't want to miss it, do you? Get over there,' she chided her nephew tenderly. 'Forget about him!'

Dorian puffed in faux offence. 'Rude!'

Jalen was visibly torn between work and play.

'Go…' Damica took charge of the ice-cream potion. 'I'll take care of him for you.'

'Give him two and a half dollops only.' Jalen gave her strict orders, accentuating the syllables of the required amount. Testing her listening skills, he lobbed his orders at her again, remixed as a quickfire exam question. 'Two and a half what…?'

'Dollops.'

She passed with flying colours.

Jalen rotated his legs out of the picnic table's legroom gap and careened towards the queue for the simulator, conjuring up a mini tornado of sand as he went. When he rejoined his new friends, a Club Enfant staff member plonked a helmet on Jalen's head and buckled the straps under his chin.

Dorian's fall hadn't been in vain. To commemorate his plummet the kids were being suited up with extra protective gear—which pleased Damica and the other carers.

Ravi angrily planted himself in the space Jalen had vacated. The wooden picnic table reverberated under his weight. Like Dorian's, the bodyguard's clothes and hair were saturated. He hadn't taken the occurrence in good humour. Obviously, he had no reason to.

Under the table, she felt Dorian brace a defensive hand on her knee. First the jungle dash, and now *this*? They awaited Ravi's reaction. A strong-worded lecture, perhaps?

Damica forecast being verbally struck down by a surge of epithets. She was well acquainted with this pattern because of her mother, to the point that she had become an active contributor in the cycle.

Act up. Get screamed at. Scream back. Be iced out. Repeat.

Soon Damica had mastered the art of instigating the 'act up' phase. That way, she was usually ahead of the curve. Being shouted at wasn't so bad when she knew that she owned the keys to her own misfortune.

Admittedly, she'd been caught off guard by her impact on Dorian's devil-may-care attitude of late. Nevertheless, Damica was tensed and ready to retaliate with her own unique brand of insults. The trick was to be so weirdly specific that their creation became a fun game, detracting from her wounded feelings.

Dorian must have sensed how strained she was feeling. His palm glided higher, rubbing soothing circles on her thigh. Meanwhile, he unleashed a word-vomit to shatter the icy quiet.

'Ravi, if you're going to assign blame to anyone let it be me, and me alone. I understand you may be nervous about your job security should this attract any media attention, but—'

'Fortunately, the press are prohibited from this

resort, so the odds of that happening are low.'
Ravi addressed them both in a slow, monotonous
manner. 'I won't waste my breath on lambasting
you, Your Highness. I don't have the jurisdiction,
after all. But I had hoped you at least respected
me—and yourself—enough to act responsibly.
I see now that I was deeply wrong on that account. That is all.'

Giving them the cold shoulder, he positioned
himself in a way that exiled Damica and Dorian
to the outermost range of his sight.

There was a sharp intake of breath from
Dorian that Damica distinguished as lethal.
Genuine disappointment from her mother had
always been deadlier than rage. Fury came in
short bursts that she could always duck and out-
manoeuvre. Being the cause of genuine dismay
had far greater haunting power. It made her re-
evaluate her ethics and shamefully conclude that
the end rarely justified the means.

On no account was the relationship between
Dorian and his bodyguard one of equal footing to her and her mother. But upsetting the
man he'd peacefully co-existed with for the last
twenty years was not a happy thing.

In an effort to prevent the escalation of their
confrontation into a full-out fight, Damica did
her duty and started feeding Dorian with the
melted ice cream. He'd be physically unable to

say anything he might regret if his throat was preoccupied with swallowing.

Two, three, four spoonsful. Definitely over Jalen's recommended dosage. But, hey—who was she to let free ice cream go to waste?

Damica scooped up as much lukewarm ice cream as the spoon would allow, and Dorian co-operated by opening his mouth. His tongue swirled around the dip of the curved plastic, licking it clean. The fuzzy moustache and beard outlining his cupid's bow of a mouth and his chin showcased how appetising his wet lips were. Audaciously, he held her gaze and maintained his consistent caress of her leg.

She'd assumed Dorian had initiated this tactile mode of comfort for her benefit. Although how anything this electrifying could instil calmness was beyond her. She understood now, after pondering on alternative motives, that Dorian was touching her in order to self-soothe…

That was what people who loved each other did.

Love.

But of course they had a special adoration for one another. They were friends. She didn't need to be a mind-reader to know definitively that Dorian loved her, but it was through no other channel but platonically.

Damica was fixated on the tub's contents,

scraping the corners for the very last dregs of ice cream.

'You're…um…going to be an amazing father one day,' she told him. 'It's like you're a kid-whisperer.'

The tingling pressure on her thigh vanished as Dorian let go.

Sensibility twanged back into her brain with the force of a boomerang. And since she couldn't go to her therapist, she'd have to provide psychological guidance to herself…something about self-sabotage.

Yada-yada.

She wasn't used to being 'normal' and she was having trouble adjusting. Having acclimatised herself to chaos throughout her thirty-three years of living, it made sense that she was addicted to havoc. Now that she'd retired, her neurological pathways were struggling in the absence of the dysfunction that was usually intrinsic to her very being.

In other words, she was bored and looking for a problem. Agonising over the prospect of being in love with Dorian was a self-imposed dilemma.

She'd gone from working twenty-four-seven to lazing around in paradise. No wonder her under-stimulated mind had concocted a whirlwind romance with her best friend.

'Is there a Nobel Prize for looking after kids?' she asked. 'You're probably eligible.'

And Damica didn't stop there, driving a further wedge between their contradicting lifestyles.

'The next generation of Sotiropouloses are in very capable hands.'

'I would hope so...'

She was confused by how unconfident he sounded—nonetheless, she didn't let this minor puzzlement detract from her overall aim: to give prominence to her and Dorian's lifestyle differences. There was no questioning whether he would father children. The only answer was 'yes'. Anyone with a brain knew that he had an obligation to continue, and in turn strengthen, the Sotiropoulos bloodline.

Thankfully, Damica had no such responsibility or rigid expectation.

'That's one of the things I like the most about you. How passionate you are about kids,' Damica went on. 'When you take off your crown, you can still identify exactly who you are. A man, an artist, a future dad...there's so much to choose from. At our last session, my therapist suggested that I look up some evening classes online and pick three non-performing arts subjects that interested me. But I couldn't even—'

Realising that she was rambling, and veering slightly off topic, Damica shut herself up. They were talking about Dorian—not her ongoing identity crisis.

'Everyone is someone away from their work,' he reasoned slowly. 'When I look at you, I see...'

Damica sighed at his hesitation. 'See? You can't think of anything right away.'

Dorian pushed onward. 'I see someone who loves her sister and nephew very fiercely. A loyal sibling and aunt. There are so many possibilities for you. You're stunning, and you know how to turn heads. You could start a clothing brand if you wanted to. Become a mother if you wish. Maybe combine the two with a mother-child fashion line?'

He might as well have described an alien.

She reflected on the possibility of being a mother. 'I mean, I hated being a child, so I want to make sure I have my life together before I have my own children...so they don't suffer. Whenever I do become a mom, I just want as few complications as possible. Simple conception. Simple pregnancy.'

Realistically speaking, Damica was aware that 'parenthood' and 'simplicity' was an oxymoron. She'd experienced the struggles of motherhood second-hand, when she'd been commodified at a young age in order to provide for her entire family.

'What are your opinions on IVF?' Dorian asked.

Case in point. Not all parents could conceive naturally.

'That's definitely something to consider. A couple of years back a friend of mine had IVF… it put so much stress on her body. And don't even get me started on the relationship with her partner. My heart goes out to everyone undergoing the procedure. It's tough. I don't think I could do it. I know the whole adoption process is tricky, but I think I would try that.'

Damica stopped twiddling with the empty ice cream pot and spoon. Braving a brief look over at Dorian, she was relieved to discover that he wasn't paying attention to her. Whilst towelling down his hair, he was watching the kids taking turns on the simulator. His expression was a mixed palette. The frown lines etched around his mouth harboured loathing, while hurt pooled in his pupils.

'There's a law back at home that excludes adopted royals from the line of succession.'

Blood purity. Another feature of the institutional beast that was royalty.

Some monsters should not be tolerated, only slayed… What did Dorian's readiness to dance with this particular dragon for the rest of his life say about him? And what did her entire friendship with Dorian say about her? Was she indirectly endorsing bigotry?

Damica curbed her interrogation before her identity issues spiralled into a morality crisis, but she did ask, 'Can the law be abolished?'

'Royalty and politics are an ever-changing game. Cut off the head, and three more the same will grow from the wound.' With his words, Dorian painted an image of bleak resignation. 'Even if the law were to be rightfully changed, the media and the royalists would still never let the adoptee forget their origins. I would hate to expose any child to that. Every child should be loved and embraced, regardless of their biological parentage.'

'Does it ever scare you? How much power you'll have as a king…and as a dad?'

'All the time.'

'One missed Christmas recital and *boom*! Your kid'll have low self-esteem and commitment issues for life,' Damica quipped, keeping her tone light and airy. 'I think we'll do a better job with our children, though. Our parents gave us a masterclass of what *not* to do, right?'

'Right.'

Dorian's lips twisted into a mournful shape, triggering another crop of confusion to come creeping back into her. This recurring strain was more potent. New questions arose. She'd thought Dorian liked children—so why was he so saddened by her mention of him raising his own. How could he be saddened about something that should make him happy? Or perhaps it was her ambiguous phrasing that had unsettled him?

By 'our children', she hadn't really meant *their*

children. Obviously Dorian would have no romantic future with her…

Here she was *again*…manufacturing her own unrest.

Determined to exterminate the weird energy between them, she decided to muster up the courage to ask him what was wrong.

Now or never. Put it all on the proverbial table. Better to speak your piece than wallow in silence, right?

She gave herself that mini pep-talk and then drummed her nervous fists on the wooden surface of the picnic table. Just as she was about to verbalise everything, Dorian got to his feet.

Jalen's turn on the simulator was calling for a standing ovation.

Like a proud father, Dorian whipped his mobile phone out of the pocket of his swim trunks. It was a miracle that the device could still function in the wake of such a crash as he'd had, but the cracked screen blinked into life under the bossy flick of his finger. After another flurry of swipes, Dorian was filming Jalen's first steps onto the blue slope in pursuit of the fixed surfboard.

Pushing aside her inquisitiveness, Damica stood up to join Dorian in his overt support of Jalen. Seemingly his weirdness over the possibility of having his own kids had vanished. Maybe she'd been overthinking, over-analysing and over-hypothesising and there had been nothing wrong to begin with…

Noticing the two adults eagerly awaiting his simulator debut, Jalen sent them a giddy wave. Damica returned his greeting, just as Dorian threw him a thumbs-up.

'Here we go…'

Dorian was watching Jalen with the kind of intensity that Hollywood directors reserved for blockbusters. She'd definitely been reading too much into his behaviour. The saying *If it ain't broke don't fix it* was especially fitting for this occasion. Dorian's excitement over Jalen was so…wholesome. Their time together at the resort was warm, soft and safe, an escape away from the world's problems, and Damica owed herself some peace too.

So she wouldn't burst her own bubble by conjuring up wild scenarios and romantic feelings for Dorian.

Age Fifteen

From: mrdoryfish7@inbox.com
To: damidiamondzzz@inbox.com
Re: Hmm… Part Two

Hi Damica,
I like your use of simile, especially when comparing yourself to a bird that must fly away to freedom. It's very effective.

There's a full breakdown of my thoughts in the attachments. I'm honoured that you wanted to share this with me. Hopefully, I didn't go overboard with the analysing...

It's just that, in a way, reading poetry and creative writing sort of reminds me of my mother. I don't remember much, because she died when I was so young. The memories of her reading to me before bed have always stayed with me, though.

Nowadays, I find myself thinking about her a lot. About what she would think of me.

Sometimes I fear she would be ashamed of me, like the people of my country seem to be.

The whole reason I joined in with the drinking in the first place was because I wanted to forget the trip Father and I took to England during the school break. Coincidentally, we went to London. Don't worry...you didn't miss anything amazing. Although Madame Tussaud's is cool if you avoid your own wax model.

Then we stayed with a family friend in the countryside who is a big fan of hunting. Him and Dad failed to tell me about the initiation ritual they perform on first-timers, where they dunk their heads into the belly of a fresh deer corpse...

It didn't matter how many showers I took or how much I brushed my teeth that night. Whenever I closed my eyes there was blood blocking my nose and mouth all over again.

I've thought about telling the school counsellor this... Did I mention before that school has made me have sessions with her? But even though she's nice, and lets me sit there in silence, I just can't trust her. When I have a child, I don't want things to be like that between us. I want them to feel free enough to speak with me about whatever they wish. Anything.

And there'll be no hunting and dead animals for us. No...every summer we'll take a trip to the coast, where we'll ride on our bikes near the sea and eat ice cream sandwiches for dinner.

Also, you are right! I can't stand *Keep your head up*. It's right up there with *Stay strong*.

From,
Dorian

From: damidiamondzzz@inbox.com
To: mrdoryfish7@inbox.com

Dear Dorian,
Ooh, yeah!
    XD
Stay strong... Keep your head up... And the final boss... *I'm always here if you ever need someone to talk to.*

I had to go to appointments with a therapist too, around the time Dad popped back into my life. Did your therapist give you that little speech about having to tell your parent if they thought you were a danger to yourself or others?

I've never thought about doing anything like that, but when I found out that she could snitch on me to Mom I knew I'd never be able to open up. I could just imagine how everything would go wrong if I didn't say the right thing. She'd tell Mom. Feir Channel would find out somehow, and they'd put out all these statements to the media, and even more people than before would be talking about it and it would never stop.

When I'm not on stage I just wanna be invisible. All the comments never stop, and I wish they would.

Thank you for making time for me and taking notes on my song. This means a lot!

I know we've been joking about hating all these phrases...but the hunting story and all the blood sounds like a scene from a horror movie. I hope you're okay now?

<3

Your future kid is gonna be so lucky to have you. If I think hard enough, I can see myself with a daughter. Always a little girl, for some reason. And we're wearing matching tracksuits.

:D

From,

Dami

From: mrdoryfish7@inbox.com
To: damidiamondzzz@inbox.com

Dear Dami,

Thanks for asking. I think I'm doing all right now. There's so much to do here, so I don't have much time to remember it any more. I can't decide if the situation was more mortifying than frightening.

Yes, the school counsellor gave me the same warning.

Honestly, my death would only attract more attention to me. When my mother passed, people spoke about her so much it felt like she was still living. There were pictures of her everywhere too, from the palace to literally every street in Concarre.

Time travel doesn't exist, for obvious reasons. However, I like to think there was true peace in the moments before I was ever created. I simply didn't exist. No name. No cells. Nothing. So there was nothing to criticise or pick apart.

If I could, I'd go back to that.

The downside would be that I couldn't eat my grandmother's *yazdi* cakes ever again, or get to see the *Mona Lisa* in person. We wouldn't have met either. So maybe not...

Message me whenever you want. It's always good to hear your thoughts. Doesn't matter if it's in an email or in a song.

Cheers,
Dorian

CHAPTER SIX

DAMICA LET OUT another aggravated sigh. Never in his life had Dorian heard so many expressions of frustration in the timespan of just thirty minutes.

'This requires patience…' he assured her in a low tone, inclining his bent head towards her whilst maintaining the steadiness of his fingers. 'You'll get the hang of it.'

'Easy for you to say.'

Dorian peeped upwards, in time to see her casting a cynical glare on his growing collection of artfully folded palm leaves. Baskets. Crowns. Animals. You name it—Dorian had made it.

'You're naturally good at this,' she told him.

Clearly giving up hope, Damica released her grip on whatever it was she was trying to construct. Its formation only survived for a few seconds, before unravelling into a chaotic mass of glossy green leaves, with points sticking up at various angles. Her shoulders slouched in defeat.

They were stationed in a quiet corner of the

Club Enfant house, on the outskirts of one of the kids' afternoon craft sessions.

Following his embarrassing fall on the surfing simulator a couple of days prior, Dorian had been forced to apply some structure to his life on the resort. Mornings were dedicated to physical activities—swimming, scuba diving, playing tennis over on a different island and the like. Afternoons were for creative and intellectual enrichment—hence this designated arts and crafts time.

By the time the evening rolled around their minds were stuffed with brand-new experiences and everyone was ready to progress to dinner. 'Everyone' being himself, Jalen and Damica.

Their collective company had become a lifeline for Dorian. Now that he was tasting the fruits of domesticity, he could no longer comprehend how he'd survived the clinical confines of his royal upbringing. Existence within this imitation of a functional family unit was so utterly blissful that he knew returning to normal was destined to come with astounding withdrawal symptoms.

Dorian abandoned his latest creation—an incomplete fish—in favour of picking up Damica's work. Cupping it in both of his hands, he carefully lifted the tangled leaves up.

'A unique specimen…full of character and life…nowhere near as bad as you think.'

In response to this glowing review, Damica raised a perfectly arched eyebrow and crossed her arms. She echoed his description dryly. *'"Full of character"?'*

Dorian almost burst out laughing. 'Yes.'

'That's a nice way of saying it's shi—*bad*.'

Remembering she was within a shared radius with children, Damica censored her use of a rude word. Ravi's scowl of disapproval from a few seats away was confirmation that she was in danger of being overheard.

'Bad,' Damica insisted.

'I don't think that at all,' Dorian said. 'I'm being one hundred percent truthful.'

He was. In all honesty, he didn't think he possessed the discipline nor the conviction to classify any of her actions as negative, because he'd grown so infatuated with her. He knew better than to admit such an affliction aloud, though.

'Since you're an artistic guru, tell me what I was making, then, O Wise One.' Damica's sarcasm strengthened.

But Dorian wasn't the type of person who gave away an upper hand without putting up a fight.

'A car…obviously,' he retorted arrogantly.

Damica's eyes widened. 'Wow…'

Wow, indeed.

Her expression magnified the upward slant of her eyes and the marble-white of her sclera. Had her irises always been this mesmerising? Dark brown wasn't the right categorisation for their colour. No, it was a rare, complex hue that bordered obsidian. And her eyelashes… Each and every hair was naturally arranged in a way that reminded Dorian of delicate flower petals. Awe-inspiring by design.

His drawing hadn't done her justice.

'Wrong.' For added effect, Damica mimicked the sound of an error buzzer.

'Ah…' Dorian swallowed, zooming out of his fantasy. 'I see your intended vision now…'

'Which is…?'

'An…insect.'

Another buzzer sounded. 'Wrong again.'

'All this secrecy is killing me. Enlighten me.'

Damica plucked the knotted mess of palm leaves away from Dorian. 'It's a bird!'

'Ah. Right…' He knew the winged creatures had always held so much significance for her.

'I'm gonna have to throw it away,' she said.

'No, don't. It's fixable.'

Dorian quickly hooked his ankle around one of the legs of the kid-sized chair he'd had to contort himself to sit on. Scooting himself closer to Damica, who also dwarfed her seat, Dorian calmly slid his hands over hers. Under his touch, she went still. No longer prodding at the palm leaves, she stared down at the way their fingers worked together.

'If you fold this part through here…just like that… Perfect!'

Dorian whispered his instructions and they worked together to restore life to the mangled palm leaf bird. Damica's skin felt soft and addictively smooth under his fingers. Cool too. The ceiling fan was whirling on its highest setting, and in conjunction with the ocean breeze emanating from the open set of double doors it created a chilly haven. The swaying curtains, Ravi's gloom and the cacophony of childish squawks not far off seemed to dim, unable to compete with the centre of Dorian's activity.

As the restored bird took new form, Damica's nose scrunched up. A troop of wrinkles gathered at her T-zone, turning her attentiveness into the world's greatest show. Just like when she'd been surfing, the tip of her tongue made an appearance. She was in the zone, and Dorian was a charmed spectator.

He helped her weave the palms until she got the hang of it on her own. 'Good…there you go…'

'You're good with your hands,' she whispered.

He conveyed his agreement by absentmindedly trailing a fingertip from her wrist to her knuckle. The deft graze elicited an involuntary shiver from Damica that threw Dorian off-kilter—more violently than the simulator. Back then, he'd had a brush with possible concussion at worst. Right here, right now, with both his feet on solid ground, Dorian was hit with a truth much more disorientating.

This was the closest he would ever get to consummating his attraction towards Damica. He'd been deluding himself into thinking he was loving this mirage of stolen touches and lingering looks. In actuality he was pushing down his desire for more and clinging to their friendship because he was deathly afraid.

Everything between them was destined to change should he open up about his uncertain ability to procreate. All it would take was a confession about his compromised sperm and her nose-scrunching would become an indication of disgust.

Dorian was no seer or fortune-teller—he didn't have to be, because most of his social scripts were highly predictable. If he'd learnt anything from his father's diatribes, it was that being 'a real man' came with a lot of expectations and preconceived ideas. Yes, he might feel the pressures of prince hood were eliminated when he was with Damica and Jalen. Yes, they stripped back his royal armour and afforded him humanity... But underneath it all he was still a *man*. And, as stereotypical as it was, Dorian found that he enjoyed providing for Damica.

A calculated guess had led him to assume that she had a set of rigid characteristics she found attractive in potential partners…just because most people did. Wasn't all attraction discriminatory and inflexible to some degree? Would she bend her rules for him?

His inner realist had reached the conclusion of a resounding *no*. All the open-mindedness that carried their friendship would drain away should they decide to open the bedroom door, and Dorian didn't want to be anywhere else other than in her high regard. He'd lost her once, and he couldn't bear to lose her again.

Oblivious, Damica let go of him so she could marvel at their finished product: a proper bird. A defined beak and tail feathers jutted out proudly on opposite sides of a body in a series of inter-connected triangles and angles.

'Look at this beauty!' she exclaimed. 'It's definitely a *her*. I'm gonna call her Birdy—subject to change.'

Fishing around in a nearby bowl, Damica rummaged for a pair of googly eyes.

Dorian schooled his expression to conceal his inner anguish. 'See? Never doubt the Guru.'

Even in an alternative timeline, where she reciprocated his feelings and became a royal bride, he knew they would still struggle. Damica's opinions of pregnancy and having a family had imprinted themselves into his memory. She wanted to conceive and raise her children under easy circumstances—understandable,

given her childhood. Dorian could never grant
her those wishes. There would be little rest or re-
spite for the woman *he* married. Her body would
be poked at and fiddled with until she was able
to conceive and carry a royal heir to full term.
And Dorian's fertility issues would make the
journey more difficult.

He was aware that he was galloping leaps and
bounds ahead, but nevertheless it was necessary
to cull any inklings of hope before they grew
lives of their own. Embarking down a romantic
avenue with Damica was a lose-lose situation.
All possible roads led to despair.

Damica, who'd finished dabbing PVA glue on
Birdy's face and sticking down the eyes, fanned
the bird with her hands in hopes of speeding
up the drying process. Dorian scraped his chair
back to its original place, although really he
wanted to join in with the flapping. Mainly on
the off-chance that their skin would touch briefly
in passing. Being near Damica was a sure way
to bring him comfort and help him communicate the many things he could never say aloud.

Whether or not she understood this new language was a mystery to Dorian. And, honestly,
he'd come to favour this wondering status above
the confirmed rejection that awaited him on the
other side of this unverified limbo.

More pressing matters barged their way to the

forefront of his mind. 'I have something to tell you,' he told her.

'Okay...' Damica slowed her movements as if in anticipation of his news.

'I might have...' He threw himself headfirst into building suspense, dragging out the pause. 'Volunteered us...as chaperones for the Club Enfant party...tomorrow night.'

'Chaperoning? Us as chaperones?'

Damica tested the responsibility as though she was trying on a dress. A doubtful scoff from Ravi notified them both that the eavesdropping bodyguard thought they were an ill fit for the job.

'I don't know... This is pretty short notice.'

Dorian sheepishly acknowledged that. 'I was feeling spontaneous. And Jalen was upset when you told him he couldn't go I thought it would make things easier for you to let him go, knowing that you can watch him the whole time.'

The celebration had been strategically scheduled to take place during the early evening, freeing carers and parents to explore the post-sundown entertainment the resort had to offer. Damica's reservations stemmed from the party coinciding with Jalen's bedtime.

Damica's hands dropped into her lap, further proving her astonishment. 'You're spoiling him too much.'

'I can't help it.' Dorian shrugged. 'Plus, if I

recall correctly—which I always do—you've always wanted to go to a school dance.'

She shook her head in amusement. 'We're on a summer vacation…'

'With some *school-aged* children,' Dorian pointed out. 'Let's use our imaginations.'

'I…' Damica looked around, as if seeking justification for why she should deny herself excitement and finding none. 'Fine.'

Asking her to dine under the stars with him—and Ravi—whilst a private band serenaded them was obviously out of the question, but appeasing their childhood selves was harmless, thought Dorian. *Healthy*, in fact.

'Spectacular. I'll stop by your villa, so we can walk over together.'

Damica would have been maddened by Dorian's short notice if not for her increasing inability to stay angry with him and her long-time love of impulsivity.

Double Dare was the name of her highest-selling album for a reason: partying had been an authentic part of her brand and her being. A sheltered and fun-deprived adolescence had evolved into a hedonistic regime that had conquered her twenties. But tonight, at thirty-three years old, she was ready—and ironically better equipped—to fulfil her childhood wants.

'Can we go now, Auntie Dami? Is Dorian here yet?' Jalen tugged impatiently on her skirt.

She prised his fingers away from the tassels and patted his shoulder. 'Not yet.'

Unable to curb his excitement, the boy spun around. His small, sandalled feet tapped against the villa floor in a summoning rhythm and his blazer-clad arms performed what looked like an obscure form of wizardry. The mismatch in his dress style was self-inflicted, and the result of a last-minute shop at the resort boutique. The party had no dress code, but the formality of hunting new attire was a game that both nephew and aunt had enjoyed playing.

Jalen paused to alter the angle of his bowtie. 'How about now?' He pressed her for an update.

'He's on his way, Jalen.' Damica smiled. 'Be patient.'

'Boo!'

Jalen gave a thumbs-down signal, then jogged towards the living room for instant gratification from his favourite cartoons. He passed his mother, Taylor, in the doorway, and acquiesced to a hug and a kiss before disappearing.

'Thank you…*thank you…thank you.*' Damica's youngest and only sister pecked her cheek in the middle of her dash to the hall mirror. Using her reflection as a guide, Taylor put on a pair of gigantic hoop earrings.

'I'd say don't stay up too late…' Damica told

her. 'But that's the entire point of me taking Jalen to the kids' party.'

Her consciousness diverted to her own evening plans with her husband, Taylor shouted, 'Babe! Hurry up! We're already late for the show!'

A gravelly voice hollered back something indecipherable, and the toilet in their shared bathroom was flushed.

In the oval looking glass, Taylor's winged-eyeliner-framed gaze fluttered to Damica. 'Are you sure you don't wanna come with us? We've barely seen each other this entire vacay. Dorian's welcome to tag along…'

'Positive.'

Damica had given up wondering whether her sister's string of invitations was being extended out of kindness or guilt—remorse for saddling the sister who'd already singlehandedly financed her whole life with her son.

Their relationship had never been conflict-proof. But Damica was now forthcoming enough to confront how she'd envied Taylor's freedom. Fame had meant she'd missed out on birthdays, funerals, graduations… Her sister had got to have the kind of life that Damica never could. Looking after Jalen on this holiday wasn't enough to replenish the empty well of experience, but Damica was being nourished by the quality time she'd accumulated with her nephew.

She was also learning that taking care of a child was no walk in the park, and that parents needed a break sometimes.

Leroy hurried into the hall, zipping up his trouser fly and making a beeline for the door. Following her husband's lead, Taylor grabbed her leather shoulder bag and shoved an arm through the chain strap. Her high heels clicked at irregular intervals.

'Text me if you need me. I *swear* I'll drop everything in a heartbeat—'

'We'll be fine, Tay,' Damica vowed, straining against the nerves bubbling in the pit of her stomach like a soft drink fizzing with an abundance of carbon dioxide.

Her tone was honeyed, but she knew the evening was full of explosive potential. She didn't know which particular phenomenon to ascribe this exhilaration to: Dorian's impending arrival or the general itinerary of the evening ahead…?

Better to leave this particular stone unturned, she concluded.

Leroy leaned around Taylor's frantic gestures to give Damica a tight-lipped smile and a cordial wave. Then he opened the door…to reveal Dorian.

The commotion of bodies took a while to clear, but greetings served dually as farewells and Damica's party moved aside to let her sibling and brother-in-law exit the villa. It wasn't until

Damica neared the now unobstructed doorway that she got a better view of Dorian.

His style was just the right balance of smart and casual. The crisp fit of his jacket accentuated the lines of his shoulders, and the dark material made the loud pattern of his Hawaiian shirt and the twinkle of his favourite gold necklace stand out.

Those tender hands were outstretched, with a bouquet and a roll of paper in them.

The airways in Damica's lungs constricted at the sight of the ornate cluster of folded palm roses.

'Dorian…' She was almost at a complete loss for words. 'This is… *Thank you.*'

Damica took the bouquet from him, blaming the tremble caused by their overlapping skin on an imaginary post-sunset chill and the convenient timing of Jalen whooshing past.

Dorian handcrafting her flowers was a gift all on its own, but her wonder expanded once she'd unfurled the accompanying tube of paper. Its firm texture and contents confirmed her suspicion that the sheet had been extracted from some kind of sketchbook.

'Dorian! You're here!'

The four-year-old launched himself at his grown-up friend. Meeting him halfway, Dorian crouched down to pick him up. With Jalen's legs wrapped around his midsection and his arms

locked around his neck, Dorian ascended back
to his full height. Hoisting Jalen up higher, he
provided the child with extra support by closing
a secure arm around his waist.

They exchanged some words, but Damica was
too enchanted by the flowers and the detailed
drawing to listen in. In her hand, the whirls and
grooves of ivory leaves merged into green, as
though visually representing the contentment
suffusing her system. The leaves on the curled
page housed a heart-warming group portrait fea-
turing herself, Dorian and Jalen.

Every possible shade of pencil had been ex-
ploited, from the dark hue of everyone's textured
hair to the glint that completed all three smiles.
The result was a near-3D creation of the treasure
hunt adventure's ending.

Jalen sat atop Dorian's shoulders, preserved
mid-cheer and pumping a small fist. Dorian
was holding on to Jalen's thighs, his mouth was
twisted into a wolfish shape that mirrored a pirate's growl, and his pupils were angled sideways, tracking directly to where Damica was
standing beside them.

Her head was thrown back in amusement,
connected to her stretching neck adorned with
stylish veins. The hand she rested on her stomach appeared to be a placement to contain hys-
terical laughter. Through Dorian's eyes and
under the tip of his pencil she looked positively

radiant—nothing like the sweaty mess who had run around the resort's jungle island for an afternoon.

Damica had seen Dorian bestow life upon a plethora of artwork countless times, but this… this was special. For her specifically.

She surfaced from her deep-dive inspection— only to nearly drown in the unnamed intensity pooled in Dorian's stare.

Detaching herself quickly, Damica brandished the palm leaf rose bouquet and the drawing at him. 'I hate it that I don't have a vase or a frame to display these in. They're stunning— I'm stunned!'

'That you have something I've made is enough.' One side of Dorian's mouth was weighed down in humility, making a lopsided smile that nurtured her happy buzz.

Damica laid the flower arrangement on the hall dresser, then melted back into his vicinity to address the child so at home in his arms.

'Jalen, look. Isn't this cool?' She pinched the corners of the curled paper between her fingertips and held it up for the boy to view.

Jalen gasped in fascination at his likeness translated into art. Eyes bright, he relived his treasure hunt fame with a bent arm and a celebratory swing of his fist. 'Argh!'

The trio chuckled harmoniously at Jalen's pirate impression.

Spreading the joy, Dorian chipped in with, 'Yarr! Shiver me timbers!'

Wild expressions replaced his handsomeness with a goofy distortion that only compelled Damica to admire him even more. It seemed fitting that a man so in tune with his own silliness and creativity had the power to present her with the most beautiful drawing she had ever seen.

For Damica, the world's finest jewels were relatively easy to come by. If she wanted them, all she had to do was make a phone call. Dorian's gifts to her were uniquely cultivated, with a type of care that money could never buy. And tonight he was granting her the most priceless gift of them all: the coming-of-age experience that she'd never got to have in real time.

CHAPTER SEVEN

DAMICA MIGHT HAVE been physically standing with Dorian, but he knew that she was mentally elsewhere.

The Club Enfant clubhouse had undergone a makeover. Gone were the majority of the tables used for craft activities and workshops. The survivors had been renovated into a home for paper plates, stacked plastic cups, punch bowls and a snack spread that put the resort buffets to shame.

The surface of the tropical fruit punch rippled, retaliating against the obnoxiously loud Y2K-inspired pop tune pouring out from the coordinated speakers perched at each corner of the room. The dance floor was swimming with young partygoers no older than ten years of age. Their small statures were deceiving. Teeming with sugar, they aggressively danced and threw shapes—shapes Dorian hadn't even known existed—under a sheet of gossamer lights projected from the disco ball hanging overhead.

Although Dorian considered himself a competent caregiver, this party was turning into a bootcamp in the art of patience. When the kids weren't crying, they were arguing. If they weren't arguing, they were running around at a zillion miles per hour. Truth be told, he'd severely miscalculated the difficulty level of being chaperone. His well-thought-out surprise for Damica had devolved into... Well...*this*... He couldn't fault her for withdrawing.

Their spot on the dance floor's perimeter gave them a comprehensive view of the vicinity. A damp patchwork of paper towels marked the spot where a boy had vomited up his sausage rolls an hour prior. Another chaperone was battling against the clock to escort a girl to the bathroom before she peed herself. Mere feet away a group of children were squabbling amongst themselves over the correct moves for some TikTok dance routine. Damica was hugging herself as she observed them rehearsing.

As if aware of Dorian's quizzical glances, she grinned over at him. Alas, her smile was dimmer than the shimmering gold of her dress, which was a telltale sign of her waning happiness.

He needed to fix this.

Immediately.

Promptly, his hand gravitated towards hers like a moth drawn to a flame. 'Come with me.'

The snug fit of their interlocking fingers administered a welcome rush to Dorian's bloodstream, and he indicated for Ravi to track them from a distance.

Damica's gaze ricocheted between the compliant bodyguard and his prince. 'What's…?'

'You'll see.'

Dorian withdrew from the party, pulling back to the very edge of the sidelines until his back met the closed double doors. Giving the handle a testing rattle, he held down the lever and pushed until one of the doors opened. Its creak was smothered by the music and bustling celebration.

Trust me, he mouthed at Damica.

Still holding on to him, she followed.

The two of them slipped out into the night. The cool air and the dramatic dip in noise welcomed them like a delayed exhalation.

Dorian led her across the small garden area, squeezing her fingers persuasively. Together they navigated the obstacle course of discarded toys and swept aside the low-hanging leaves frilling the quiet pathway leading to the nearest beach. The lulling *shush* of the ocean waves steered them through the darkness, and the view that opened up was even more tranquil.

A deserted beach awaited them. The moon was comfortably posted at the sky's pinnacle, reigning over the scattering of stars. Its light reflected sharply off the sea's breadth and illuminated the safe passage of damp sand.

Dorian paused, allowing Damica to take in the breathtaking scene. 'I thought this might make you feel better.'

'Thank you… But I'm fine,' she mumbled.

Dorian was unconvinced. He released her hand and moved to stand directly in front of her. Spreading his arms elaborately, he took up all the space of her visual field, making himself impossible to ignore.

Damica crossed her arms and tossed him a scowl. 'What are you doing?'

As usual, her nose was scrunching up, as if in distaste. But Dorian knew it was mostly for show this time around.

He lobbed a disarming smile her way, kicking off his loafers and saluting the soft, grainy sand with his bare feet by curling his toes. Without removing his eyes from Damica's, Dorian jogged backwards, using nothing but his intuition to move himself to the heart of the shore. The party's playlist of current songs had been reduced to a distant memory, its replacement the never-ending hush of waves.

That was good enough for them. Perfect, actually.

'Come and dance with me!' he called, presenting his hand.

She didn't shout back…which technically wasn't a rejection.

Dorian waited. Waited so long that an ache

started to build in his arm muscles—biceps, triceps and company.

From where he stood, Damica's form looked no larger than a toy figurine. Nonetheless, he was positive he could see the tension bleeding out of her shoulders and her armour cracking inch by inch. As she drew closer, she grew larger. She stopped briefly to dispose of her shoes, flinging her high heels onto the shore. Confidence clearly increasing, she broke into an easy run.

Her long braids streamed out behind her as she hurried over to him. Her gold fringed mini dress sparkled and glimmered in solidarity with the moonlight, which bathed her in a delicate glow. Meanwhile the stretch and brightness of her smile eclipsed the stars. She was free. She was breathtakingly beautiful. She was...*his*.

All his.

And he was in love with her.

In tandem with his realisation Damica crashed into Dorian with a hug that sent him staggering backwards.

'Okay...maybe you're right. I do feel better now!'

The unfiltered and slightly unhinged pitch of Damica's laugh occupied his entire ear as he fought to reassert his physical and cognitive stability. Although with her pressed up against him so intimately, Dorian was a lone soldier in a losing battle.

Once he was firmly upright, he returned her embrace by circling his arms around her waist.

Dancing, he reminded himself. *They were meant to be dancing.*

Dorian swayed hesitantly, and Damica joined in with his awkward movement. She incorporated her feet into the sequence, so soon they were stepping from side to side, making a tentative rhythm of their own.

Damica hung her head, pretending to monitor their uncertain legs. But Dorian had already noticed the dwindling magnitude of her smile.

'My first time at a school dance. Am I doing this right?' she asked sardonically. 'The closest I've been to one of these things is the *Dani DoRight* prom episode.'

'There are no rules,' he promised, his lips purposefully skirting along her earlobe.

Damica's rhythm lost momentum for a split-second, but she covered up the falter by wrapping her arms around him even tighter.

'If it's any consolation, I spilled punch all over my shirt at my first dance,' he told her.

She gasped sympathetically. And because their chests were pinned together, Dorian felt Damica's sharp intake of breath and the press of her breasts when she exhaled. The sensation

bulldozed through his declining sense of awareness.

Easing his touch lower, Dorian let his hands
find a new home at the flare of her hips. He was
suddenly a teenager again, experiencing his first
foray into romance. His heart was ratcheting inside him, threatening to burst free of the ana-
tomical tissue holding the vital organ in place.

Growing bolder, he rested his chin on Damica's shoulder and let one of his palms ascend to
the bare slope of her exposed back. She arched
into him, causing him to raise his head.

'Should I stop…?'

Before he could lift his head she raked a hand
through his hair, her nails grazing his scalp. The
encouragement spurred his second dive—this
time his face burrowing into the connection
where her neck and shoulder met. She let out a
loud, shaky breath as his nose trailed up the col-
umn of her throat, relishing the delectable scent
of her perfume—an exclusive personalised fragrance he'd come to know.

Under the resting place of his lips, her pulse
point hammered in arousal.

All Dorian had to do was move his mouth up
a few inches.

His breath ghosted over Damica's jawline and
chin, stopping at her lips. 'And now…?'

They came to a standstill on the sand, their
dance long forgotten. Mere slivers of space sep-

arated their closely drawn faces. Dorian could perceive his own reflection in the dark mirrors of Damica's pupils. He read in them the depths of her pining. And her panic.

He knew a kindred consternation was projected by his own gaze. For he and Damica were two souls destined to pass each other periodically but never collide permanently. Or fully.

As if suddenly caving in to her impulses, Damica smashed her mouth to his quickly.

It was over in a heartbeat. More of an impersonal peck than an exchange of intimate passion.

She kept her eyes wide open the whole time, and her trembling fingertips dug into the back of his neck. Dorian didn't dare speak or move, save for dampening his lips with his tongue to savour the rushed taste of her,

Damica's clasp resettled at the sides of his face to cup his cheeks. She kissed him again. Then once more. Another, just to be sure. Each one lasted longer than its predecessor, stamped with the similarity of their unrelenting eye contact.

Although unvoiced, they were clearly in agreement that all this could amount to was a gratifying fumble in the dark. She was a retired star with a thirst for control, and he was a black hole of monarchist baggage and fertility complications.

A match made in hell.

Dorian couldn't afford to lose his head.

But shutting his eyelids came with the risk of missing out on the entirety of…whatever this was.

He'd best make the most of it…

The experimental brush of their lips evolved into something more as their searing breath ramped up the heat. Seeking more tactile sensation, Dorian slid his desperate touch back down to the small of Damica's back and beyond. His tantalising stroke over the incline of her ass earned him an invigorating sigh.

He tilted his head to the left, to deepen their next kiss, just as Damica pitched to the right.

Her right.

In an accidental clash, their foreheads banged together. The impact of the collision reverberated through his skull with an unpleasant tremor, interrupting the synchronicity of their embrace.

Conjoined souls was out of the question, but Dorian was neither pleased nor pleasured by this painful alternative.

CHAPTER EIGHT

DAMICA WAS SEEING STARS. Disappointingly, not the orgasmic kind, but dancing lights of the dizzying, disorientating variety.

She stumbled away from Dorian, her palms flying up to bracket her throbbing forehead. Her eyelids squeezed themselves shut and she hunched forward, propping her hands on her knees. A self-protective instinct took over, instructing her to accept sanctuary at ground level and the steadiness of the Earth's core.

'I am so, so…sorry!'

'Don't be—it's fine.'

'I'm not usually so clumsy—'

'My fault too.'

'Are you—?'

'Seriously, I'm *fine*.'

Her own voice sounded so distant and cold. Was that really her snapping at Dorian?

In for four seconds. Hold for seven seconds. Release for eight seconds.

Damica religiously carried out each step of her

breathing exercises. But what use would anxiety-alleviating respiratory patterns be against almost bashing her head in? She couldn't connect the dots at this time. Nevertheless, they were fixed and familiar and difficult to get wrong.

She was messing up a lot of good things lately.

Namely, one of the only dependable friendships she'd ever had.

Dorian was rubbing her back in an effort to provide stress relief. However, his show of affection only rebooted every single nerve-ending in her body. And they collectively pushed for a continuation of her and Dorian's rushed make-out session.

Damica jerked upright, further separating herself from the source of her arousal by marching back across the sand to scout out her shoes.

'Damica…?'

Dorian was right on her heels, and she knew he wouldn't be content with anything other than definitive proof that she was fine. The after-effects of him fondling her behind still sparked down her spine. Euphoric hormones still raged through Damica's system. And she was *this close*—so close—to crumbling and dragging his mouth over hers so they could kiss some more.

Divine intervention materialised in the form of Ravi, with Jalen in his arms. The bodyguard had been posted at the opening in the palm trees that Dorian had ushered her through earlier. How much earlier exactly, she couldn't determine.

Had Ravi, the shadow that he was, been watching from the wings whilst she slipped up with Dorian? If he had, she knew they could trust him to not ask questions. Her saving grace was that Jalen was fast asleep in his arms and facing away from the beach.

Damica's face burned with shame. She'd been so lost in her lust—like a randy teenager exploring her sexuality for the very first time—that she'd neglected her responsibilities. Dorian wasn't the only person with duties. Damica had an obligation to look out for her nephew and she'd failed him.

Not wanting to forsake anything else, she slowed her steps, inviting Dorian to walk by her side. 'I think about you a lot,' she blurted out. 'More than I should.'

As much as she wanted to, Damica wasn't going to run away from this problem. Independence wasn't just fun and games—there were terms and conditions too. One of them being that *she* had to deal with the consequences of her own actions. Her mother wasn't here to pen a fake apology because Dani DoRight had been busted buying contraception with her boyfriend. Mom couldn't swoop in and fix her marriage by pushing for an annulment on the grounds that both parties had been intoxicated.

Damica had to handle this all on her own.

'I lost control of myself and… Well, *that* happened.'

Alcohol wasn't a plausible excuse. Damica was stone-cold sober. She flapped her hands about—another manifestation of her own embarrassment.

'It won't again—happen again, I mean. You're you and I'm me. It's completely one hundred percent certifiably crazy to even think we could go there with one another…'

The end of her rambling appeared on the horizon at long last. Damica resisted Dorian's heavy stare and the skim of his jacket-clad arm as he pulled ahead of her.

They'd happened upon one of her shoes. He got down on one knee to retrieve the lone silver pump.

'Certifiably crazy? Hmm…'

His rendition of her words sounded blank and detached. Plus, his lowered stance made it near-impossible to see his face. Was he in agreement? Or worse… Gosh, she hadn't *upset* him, had she?

'You are not my type,' she said. 'At all.'

Real diplomatic, Damica.

She was only digging a bigger hole for herself here.

Dorian unearthed the pricey high heel, dusting the build-up of sand off the satin before dig-

FAYE ACHEAMPONG   151

ging around inside. Stray pebbles and shells were
evicted, falling back onto the sand bed.

With him squatting at her feet, Damica felt...
inexperienced. She hated it that Dorian's consid-
eration for her footwear reminded her of Prince
Charming discovering the slipper left by Cin-
derella after the ball. Because that would make
her the Princess in this ludicrous equation.

Prim and proper? No, thank you.

'And...and I'm not the right fit for you either!'
She prattled onward.

In her peripheral vision she spied a silver heel
elsewhere on the shore. Damica slogged over to
where the first shoe's companion lay alone at
an unbothered angle. Her abrupt parting from
Dorian would end all possibility of him performing some fairytale re-enactment.

Firstly, that would be dumb. Secondly, she'd
only hobble around with one shoe on until she
sank pitifully into the sand. Her high heels were
sorely incompatible with the low-density ground.
She'd acquired this knowledge on many occasions—her girlish dash into Dorian's arms being
one of them. Ironically, the 'sinking heel' anal-
ogy applied to her and him perfectly...

Damica snatched up her other heeled pump,
granting it an apathetic excavation, then saw
Dorian sitting down several yards away, having
detected both of his loafers. After calming her-

self down, Damica traipsed back into his range and plopped down next to him.

He wasn't Prince Charming…he was just Dorian. Her best friend Dorian. A man with Daddy issues, who was born with a silver spoon in his mouth, and a curiosity that came at the expense of his own safety. He was a lot shorter than the guys Damica was typically attracted to. But more morally upstanding…sometimes boringly so. More…caring.

It wasn't till a cape-like gathering of cloth descended upon her bare shoulders that Damica realised she was shivering. Dorian styled his jacket around her upper arms so she was deeply enfolded in its warmth. Then he handed her the missing shoe.

'I wouldn't categorise that as the best kiss I've ever had,' he said. 'But you're unquestionably in contention for Most Memorable.'

Wryness tugged at the corner of his mouth, culminating in a goofy grin that made her eyes flick upward. A novel shyness had cast its net over Damica, but at least they were back to chasing up discomfort with jokes.

So…did this mean the two of them were good? She hoped so.

Ruminating on the root cause of her pooling angst, Damica could only guess it was a knee-jerk reaction to her rejection of the boxes that so many people had pressured her into. Refusal to comply had always come with a punishment. When she hadn't played her role as someone else's puppet, the would-be puppeteer had always cut ties with her in some way. Emotional or physical.

Her own father had left her for the *second* time once she'd declined to play the part of a doting daughter. Her mom had struck her down verbally for swerving out of her designated role of Family's Golden Goose. And how could Damica forget her soured reputation amongst the Feir Channel execs every time they'd been forced to remember that their favourite child star was human too?

She'd made advances towards Dorian and then changed her mind—which wasn't a crime. But that had never prevented men who felt entitled to sex from viewing denial as a whopping violation. Just because he was a good friend, it was no guarantee that he'd make an excellent lover. Damica couldn't be sure.

All the more reason why dating him was a bad idea. Another unaccounted variable.

'Better leave it as a memory, then,' Damica countered quietly, after what felt like a lifetime of silence. She fussed with the skirt of her mini dress, twirling the tassels around her nervous fingers. 'Another one will never be able to match up.'

'Can't argue with you there.'

Dorian abandoned his study of the sea and the skyline to turn his loafers upside down. A stream of sand spilled back to its origins. Late-night luminescence cast its magic over Dorian's upstretched arm, making the shadow in the inner crook of his elbow stretch to maximise the appeal of his muscles.

Damica grasped the lapels of Dorian's jacket, bunding herself up tighter with the fabric. She was content with her present state.

Dorian's arm moved down again, taking its potential to distract along with it. He regarded her closely. So closely that she was unable to assert any authority over the temperature of her cheeks, which had skyrocketed under his speechless enquiry. He zoned in on her eyebrows and hairline, to the extent that she was frustrated with herself for feeling self-conscious.

She was Damica Foye! The one and only! Men became pathetically bashful in her presence, not the other way round.

'I should get you and Jalen back to your villa,' Dorian said. 'Although after our clash of heads I think maybe I should keep you awake for another hour or so. Just to be on the safe side.'

His inspection was earnest, swaying Damica's conclusion that he was only checking to make sure she had no bumps, marks or outward signifiers of a concussion.

'Yeah, my head was knocked around a bit—

but your head's not *that* hard,' she reassured him firmly. Damica curled her fingers into a fist and gave his forehead a light, good-natured rap with her knuckles. 'Don't worry. I'm good.'

'Wow.' Dorian blinked dramatically, capturing her wrist. 'Does my being a patient under the established Dr Jalen not mean anything to you?'

'I'm sure he'd give you an A for effort...'

In unison, they turned to take note of the esteemed four-year-old clinician, who was still snoozing, uninterrupted, in Ravi's embrace.

Damica decided to make a bid for the royal bodyguard's fellowship. She would've made a beckoning signal, for emphasis, but she didn't want to risk losing the sweep of Dorian's thumb over the inside of her wrist.

'Come and sit with us?' she invited.

To both her and Dorian's surprise, Ravi acquiesced, and the stony safeguard of his demeanour prevailed as he stalked over to the open sand next to Dorian, his actual employer. Despite his large build and the sleeping forty-pound body he held, setting him up to sink into the beach's soft surface, he moved with the lithe quickness of a jaguar. It was an evolutionary step away from his previous flounders in the holiday climate.

Ravi soundlessly alighted on the spot adjacent to Dorian whilst Jalen stirred, snorted, and used his broad shoulder as a pillow. Ravi made no other move to acknowledge Damica's existence—not that she'd expected him to. But she managed to sneak a peek at him, verifying the suitability of his arms to go on supporting Jalen's bodyweight.

'Ah. I see how it is!' Dorian soothed the prickly atmosphere with a witticism. 'Can't steal my heart, so you're robbing me of a bodyguard instead.'

Under the wooing skim of his thumb, Damica's pulse skipped. Was…was Dorian *flirting* with her? She shouldn't be enjoying this. And yet…

She had her fill of the glimmer hovering in his mocha-brown eyes before taking her wrist back. Then, scooting closer, she reclined her head onto his shoulder. With ease, Dorian draped his arm around her, completing the circuit.

'Some see it as robbery,' she said. 'I see it as a loan between friends.'

She spoke into the distance, cherishing the sight of the boundary where the night sky met the ocean. She knew that, like this late-night wonder, all good things came to an end. A favourite song. The last drawn-out bites of a comfort dish. Her time here at the Étoile Privée resort with Dorian. That didn't mean she couldn't hang on to the dregs of pleasure before they drained away, though.

'I may not seem like I do, but I can hear you,' Ravi grouched.

Damica and Dorian's childishness bubbled up, producing hushed tee-hees and conspiratorial smiles. 'Sorry, Ravi,' they crooned in unison.

For now they were two kids, staying up way past their bedtimes, drunk on the milky night and the endless possibilities of their own leisure. When sleep made its rounds it would be heavy and halting. But Damica wasn't ready for this good thing with Dorian—whatever it was—to cease just yet.

Age Seventeen

From: damidiamondzzz@inbox.com
To: mrdoryfish7@inbox.com

Hey, Dorian,
You've probably already seen all the embarrassing stories about me in the news. I still can't believe how me and Liam got caught. We were super-careful. We were both wearing hoodies and sunglasses. He was in the store for five mins max and I stayed in the car the whole time.

What kind of weirdo hangs around in the condom aisle taking pics of customers?

Paula made me sign that public statement saying I'm sorry, but I'm so confused. I don't see what I've done wrong here...

We had a 'special' meeting about it and everything... All the *Dani DoRight* producers were there, some PR people, plus a load of serious people in suits who I didn't recognise. Paula, too, obviously.

I don't even remember most of what was said because it was so humiliating. Everyone in the room looked at me like I was dirty and I hated it.

Mom didn't have my back. When we got back home she gave me this long lecture about being irresponsible and putting our future in danger.

:(

Another thing that confuses me is that sex is overrated.

Whenever Liam has sex with me I mainly just lie there and wait for it to be over. It doesn't last long, but the whole time I'm thinking, Is that it? This is what all the singers sing about? What famous writers write about?

IDK...

Maybe I'm doing something wrong.

Kissing him is really fun, though!

Have you had sex yet? What's it like for you?

Dami x

From: mrdoryfish7@inbox.com
To: damidiamondzzz@inbox.com

Dami,

I'm very sorry. I hate it that you're being treated this way.

Your mother sounds a lot like my father. He

threatened to have all my paintings thrown out of the palace if I don't join a sports club. In his opinion, a king has a duty to be athletic and strong. He says no one will take a 'flowery' leader seriously. He never lets me forget.

I have an embarrassing story to share as well: I have never had sex.

When I was still living in the boys' dormitory I'd always nod my head and make the odd comment whenever the topic came up. Just enough so I didn't stand out too much. No one wanted to ask too many questions or risk upsetting me because Ravi was always nearby in a room just down the hall. Some days I'd feel like he didn't give me room to breathe. But I'd never been more grateful to have him close by then.

My friend Dario's had plenty of girlfriends... sometimes multiple at the same time. He told me that sex is better when both people are really enjoying it, and that's the only way it should be. Therefore, it sounds like you have nothing to blame yourself for.

Apparently there's this book called *The Kama Sutra*? It's supposed to help with stuff like this. Check the attachments. I've sent you pictures of the pages!

I thought I might ask Jimena to be my girlfriend. But the palace head of security showed me proof that she's been talking to journalists. So now I know that it was her who told the press about how I vomited all over her lap during our last date.

I wish I could be angry at her. But I've had so many 'friends' betray me that I'm becoming numb.

I'm happy that I have you, Dario and Ravi.

There's a girl in my English class who I might ask to the next dance, if I even decide to go. I like hearing her opinions on Sylvia Plath.

I'll let you know if anything unfolds.

Yours,

Dorian

from: damidiamondzzz@inbox.com
to: mrdoryfish7@inbox.com

Dorian!

Forget about Jimena and her loose lips. Put the books down and ask this new girl out! You're kind and funny and artistic and extremely easy to talk to, so I already know that she's gonna say yes.

:)

Thank you for those *Kama Sutra* pics.

First of all...

W. O. W.

I shouldn't have opened those attachments from your last email when I was in Hair and Make-Up. I had to lock my phone ASAP once I saw all those bodies in those positions! I was so shocked they made me spill my juice!

Luckily, I didn't ruin my outfit for the day, because then Mom would have shouted at me even more. Plus, the lady doing my hair was very understanding. I don't think she saw anything on my phone...but she also didn't look me in the eye for the rest of my time in the trailer.

Anyway, none of that is important. I've decided that I'm never going to have sex again. You're not missing out on much.

Liam broke up with me over text. He said he hasn't been asked to return to the set and that he's probably being written out of the show because of the condom thing and me.

I wish I didn't have to be here... But I've just got to keep telling myself that I'll be free after we finish filming this season. Once I'm eighteen I'll be able to do whatever TF I want. Mom will have more than enough money.

I wish I could be with you instead. School dances sound really fun! I'd be an amazing wing woman or third wheel! You are going to ask her out, right? LOL

We could dance until our feet are sore and we can't even remember your dad or my mom. And drink so much punch that we throw up everywhere. The full experience.

Now, I'm trying to imagine you dancing, but my mind's gone blank. Are you a robot dancer or a two-step kind of guy? Do you even know what those are? LOL!

Dami xxx

From: mrdoryfish7@inbox.com
To: damidiamondzzz@inbox.com

Dami,
I think the best I can do is a shoulder shimmy! Leave me alone. Not everyone is a skilled trained dancer like you!

Have you ever considered that, for me, reading books and writing to you is exciting enough? Plus, exams are coming up. I have to think about my future.

I was going to apologise for juice spillage, but since you've insulted me so much I don't think that I will.

:P

You'll be happy to know that I *did* ask the girl I was telling you about to the dance. Her name is Diana, and I think you'd really like her. This is me promising to take loads of pictures of the party, so it feels like you're right there with us, having the best time.

I've decided to keep any information about Diana from my father for as long as I possibly can. Firstly, as much as I like her, I'm not going to get my hopes up about this leading to anything more. Secondly, whenever Father knows that I'm dating someone he always finds a way to make a snide remark about us 'doing each other's make-up'.

Painting on a canvas...painting faces. They

are apparently the same thing to him. And, of course, whenever I confront him he insists that he's only joking and I'm being too sensitive. I can never win with him.

This is probably inappropriate of me to say, but I'm overjoyed that Liam isn't in your life any more. I know I'm not physically with you, but your words always felt so sad whenever you spoke of him. Similar to when you describe your mother.

Just know that I'll always support you, and I want you to be happy. Maybe, when you're finished with your show and I've completed school, we can try and meet up secretly. What do you think?

Yours,
Dorian

CHAPTER NINE

DORIAN WASN'T THE only Concarri whose inhibitions were being stripped away by the Étoile Privée resort, layer by layer. Time really did reveal all. Case in point: Ravi's ability to commentate on his prince's current condition with a degree of accuracy that hinged on invasiveness.

The sun was beating down unforgivingly on his temples and the late-morning brightness threatened to blind him. Hangovers and drug comedowns weren't valid scapegoats for this sensitivity because he hadn't consumed a single recreational substance over the last twenty-four hours. Not unless Damica's lips qualified…

Dorian slapped a mental lid over that tangent for now. His squinting eyelids flickered and, frazzled, he ran a hand through his hair, covering up the fact that he was scratching his head in confusion. Maybe he'd misheard Ravi's latest prognosis.

'Excuse me?'

'I said, you don't know what her reaction will

be until you actually tell her.' Ravi tucked his arms behind his back, casually vocalising his thoughts as if he might be talking about something insignificant. Like the weather. Not the personal life of his literal employer. 'Whatever it is you're keeping a secret from her, that is, Your Highness.'

Dorian furrowed deeper into his defensiveness. 'What…what makes you think I'm keeping a secret?'

One of Ravi's eyebrows jerked a minor fraction, and his cheek twitched.

'Am I really that obvious?' Dorian groaned.

His hand flew up to his face and he massaged his forehead. Feelings of exposure and mortification aside, he was grateful that he and Ravi's camaraderie of sorts was piecing itself back together. Especially after the disruption generated by Dorian's recently developed streak of recklessness. Given the number of bangs to the skull he'd taken during this leave of absence thus far, he needed someone to have his back.

'No. But I wouldn't be doing my job if I didn't notice these things, Your Highness,' Ravi replied, giving himself further legitimacy.

Dorian couldn't conceive of a world in which he would ever fire his bodyguard for simply doing his job effectively. Truth be told, it was impossible to consider a life without Ravi, full stop. The assignment of differing guards to the young Crown Prince had been a revolving door that he'd never liked going through. But Ravi's indefinite allocation to the end of the corridor leading to Dorian's boarding school dorm had marked a welcome delay. Using his title to influence the roster and keep Ravi as a permanent guard had been one of Dorian's first exertions of sovereign power. And he was yet to regret his choice.

Ravi gave the word 'discreet' a fresh definition. He'd seen all of Dorian's grapples with boyhood—from his sloppy first kiss with a date on the school lacrosse field to his illicit introduction to cigars—and had uttered a word to no one. By virtue of doctor-patient confidentiality, Ravi was ignorant of the ins and outs of Dorian's reproductive health. But Dorian trusted that if Ravi ever became privy to this information he would approach it with the same subtlety.

Dorian swivelled his head, working out the kinks in his neck muscles with calculation for the activity ahead.

'What Damica doesn't know won't hurt us—not that there ever will be an "us". We're just friends on a— How do the British refer to it?' He snapped his fingers. 'Ah! A lads' holiday.'

As though conjured up by the mention of her name, a low drumming started further up the pier.

The polite resolution in Ravi's next utterance

was a tip-off that this would be the last time Dorian would be hearing from him on such a topic. 'I'm not sure Miss Damica would appreciate being referred to as a "lad", Your Highness.'

The striking of flip-flops against the pier's wooden planks amped up in both tempo and loudness, as though rolling out a carpet in auditory form ahead of its owner's grand entrance.

Dorian turned to give Damica a warm reception, and she responded in kind with a modest wave. He wanted to attribute her bashfulness to their kiss, but figured the absence of her usual young, lively associate was a more realistic source.

Jalen was notably missing this morning—his parents had reclaimed custody of him for a day, and the adult pairs were switching places. Damica's sister didn't want her booked activity slots to go to waste, so as a thank-you she'd passed them on to her sibling. Being the thrill-seeker that she was, Damica had jumped at the chance to make full use of the jet ski reservation. And, ever her devotee, Dorian had concurred.

He was trying his best not to dwell on how he and Damica were effectively acting as proxies for Taylor and Leroy—a happily married couple— when last night had eliminated all prospects of them being amorous, let alone bound by wedlock. Damica had pronounced that Dorian was leagues apart from what she usually considered appealing, which had…hurt. But the reality check had been sorely needed.

'Do you want the good news first or the bad news?'

Damica curved her palm and braced it on her brow, forming a natural visor to block out the jarring sunlight. Dorian had always considered her to be pretty. But today the generous residue of her recently applied sunscreen made her dual-toned skin glisten, and her face was free of make-up, lending substance to how naturally striking she was. To class her as 'one of the lads'—or however it was that the Brits phrased it—was truly an insult to Damica's beauty.

'Surely it can't be that bad…?'

Dorian assumed a mellow approach, which should have been easy given his choice of company. Nonetheless, his insecurities were worming around under the surface of the well-put-together, well-to-do facade he was sporting.

'Well, you said it, not me…'

And Damica launched into an abridged recap of her chat with the resort dock master.

'All their jet skis are booked right now. Not really a surprise that they're so popular. Because of that, the staff can't give us a third jet ski. So we're gonna have to split two between the three of us…'

She turned to Ravi, who was readying himself

to supply his typical forewarning about procedure and whatnot.

'I know… I *know* you can't stand and watch us from the pier. And I'm guessing you and Dorian don't wanna buddy up either. So, it's gonna have to be me and Dorian sharing a jet ski and you on the other one. Ravi?'

'That's fine with me.'

Dorian nodded definitively and drew up his shoulders, trying to exude a semblance of dominance. He wasn't feeling especially majestic, but he'd resolved to fake it till he made it so. His bodyguard might be keeping tabs on his every move, but it was the Crown Prince who ultimately called all the shots. Moreover, close proximity to Damica could never score as a loss…

Moving their conversation along, he wondered aloud, 'So what's the good news, then?'

'Isn't it already obvious? We're going jet skiing… Hello?'

The excitable hand-clap and ponytail sway that coincided with Damica's chirp only added to her innate charisma. In a further burst of elation, she discarded her flip-flops and advanced to where the jet-propelled vehicles in question awaited them.

Dorian followed suit and helped her untie the ropes that were keeping those bad boys tethered to the marina. When they were done, he motioned for her to mount what was essentially the watercraft equivalent of a motorbike.

'Ladies first.'

Its design was a brash one. The sprightly red panelling on the shell was overwhelmed by its black counterparts, and the deceptive curve of the body's apex bore a strong resemblance to a shark's nose.

Damica shot Dorian a lingering smile before climbing onboard. He took to his own seat afterwards. Their seating order meant that he was positioned rather intimately behind her, with his crotch meshed against her backside and his arms around her waist.

The vehicle bobbed subtly in accordance with the tide as they bided their time until Ravi was safely aboard his solitary jet ski. Neither of them seemed to mind the delay. Damica settled back against the support of his life-jacket-barricaded chest. The pressing of their spread legs seemed to coerce her bare thighs to mingle with the nylon of his swim trunks.

The last of Dorian's practicality crumbled. The boy who had once so chivalrously assisted an unrequited crush with boarding a watercraft at this very same marina was dead and buried. His first kiss with Damica had awakened a man with alarmingly simple wants.

The primary one being Damica.

Everything else—his royal life and his doubts

about being able to conceive an heir—would have to be secondary for the time being. With Damica, anything felt possible. Why waste the opportunity to be happy with her on this holiday? For ever was impossible for them…so a short while would have to suffice.

Damica peeped back at him over her shoulder, mindful not to whack him on the nose with her braids, which were tied back into her ponytail. 'Ready?'

'Always,' he breathed, looking down pointedly at the minimal gap between their lips.

She gulped, her focus boomeranging between his suggestive gaze and his mouth. An arrogant rush of pride bloomed in his ego, but his face betrayed nothing of the inner workings of his mind.

He jutted his chin towards the jet ski's handlebars, which she was holding on to for dear life. 'I think you need to turn it on first…'

'Right. Of course…'

A dazed Damica cut off their stare-down to fish a pair of gloves out of the jet ski's glove box. With no further heads-up, she shoved the accessories on and jabbed her thumb on the vehicle's ignition.

The pair were lurched into action, zooming away from the marina in an eruption of aggressive engine revs and explosive water that unfortunately bathed Ravi.

In the midst of the thrill and the whizz Damica and Dorian seemed to morph into a single entity, concerned with screaming at the top of their lungs and chasing a high.

Gone were Dorian's father's diatribes now—because none of them were true. Dorian wasn't some feeble dweeb who substituted poetry and art for human interaction. Quite the contrary. He was a hot-blooded male who knew how to pursue a woman. He'd topped virtually every fan-voted poll relating to the world's most eligible bachelors...so he must be a lot of people's type. And pretty soon he would be Damica's.

If Damica hadn't known any better, she'd have thought that Dorian was on a top-secret mission to seduce her.

She did, though.

Know better.

In the real world they were just two friends, strolling into the resort's spa for their scheduled session with a professional masseuse. Hardly a storyline worthy of being included in a soap opera.

Nonetheless, it warmed the lining of Damica's stomach just like a comfort meal that had been cooked to perfection. And, as though fashioned to prove her wrong, the side of Dorian's hand targeted her with an accidental nudge that sent a train of tingles shooting up the stretch of her arm.

The nanosecond of skin-to-skin contact trans-

ported her back to how he'd cuddled her from
behind on the jet ski hours earlier, the intimate
press of his body and his howls in her ear fa-
cilitating her spiking adrenaline. And then she
thought back to the deserted beach the previous
night, where they'd shared those chaste, intro-
ductory pecks bathed in moonlight...

'Welcome to the Étoile Privée Spa. How can
I be of service?'

The Zillennial woman behind the podium at
the entrance addressed Damica and Dorian.

Ushering out the disturbance of her rose-
tinted daydream, Damica jumped in to explain
her and Dorian's circumstances. 'Oh—hi, we're
here for—'

The receptionist rephrased her salutation in
French, and then in German and Mandarin, and
finally Dhivehi—the national language of the
Maldives. Her oration was so well-rehearsed that
Damica almost thought she was interacting with
an automated machine.

A short phase of quiet ensued, perhaps to
make way for any requests for more translations.
When nothing else followed, Damica gave the
woman Taylor and Leroy's booking details.

A sequence of computer mouse drags, clicks
and keyboard taps played out, mismatching with
the *boduberu* drum instrumental pouring out of
the sound system. After reading the relevant in-

formation from her computer screen, the receptionist smiled accommodatingly.

'Mr and Mrs Williams. We're so glad you are able to join us. If you require a live demonstration before your session commences, our expert masseuses will be happy to assist you.'

Damica was temporarily rendered speechless. Not by the calibre of customer service—she expected nothing less with the resort's five-star rating and rave reviews. She was confused by the staff's willingness to provide a demonstration of how they did their jobs to a pair of guests.

Why would she and Dorian need a demonstration?

'I'm sorry…would you mind checking the booking. We're just having a couples' massage, right?'

'Er…yes,' the receptionist confirmed. Her eyeballs darted from left to right as she looked through the data. '"Couples' Massage Honeymoon Hands-On Package",' she read.

Recognising Damica and Dorian's bafflement, she kindly supplied them with a spectacular pitch. 'This package is designed to boost relaxation and intimacy between couples. A bespoke selection of the world's finest massage and body oils will be at your disposal, so you can be masseuse and masseur to each other. This hands-on experience is one of our most popular treatments here at the spa!'

A string of taps moved across her wrist, like temptation licking away at her self-restraint. Discerning Dorian's incessant finger as the culprit of the stimulation, Damica awarded him her full attention. He tipped his head urgently towards the closest corner of the reception area.

Damica updated the receptionist on their pending status as spa visitors. 'We'll be just one minute! Lots to talk through!'

'No problem. Take as long as you need Miss Foye—*Mrs Williams.*'

The young woman cringed at her slip-up. However, being identified took up the least of Damica's headspace. The majority of her energy was being channelled into keeping an unyielding lid over the desire stewing in the very pit of her stomach.

Her footfalls synced with Dorian's until they made it to the privacy afforded by the corner of the room.

Dorian whirled around, propping his fists on his hips as if preparing himself to get down to business. A deep frown line cleaved the centre of his brow, illustrating just how seriously he viewed this quandary.

'We can cancel if that would make you feel more comfortable,' he told her. 'I could do with a nap before dinner anyway.'

Their daylong experience was set to conclude with an evening reservation at the resort's seafood restaurant. Drawing inspiration from its menu, the outdoor dining area was daringly constructed on stilts that were planted in the ocean.

'I'm comfortable with whatever you're comfortable with.'

Damica gave him her vague answer whilst she contemplated the crossroads that represented her needs and her wants. The sensible route included the cancellation of the couples' massage, the overwater dining and the big fat cocktails that were to be thrown in for good measure. The road less travelled was more of a wildcard...

The worst-case scenario ended with Dorian's tongue down her throat. Which wasn't really a negative at all. Was it?

With an absentminded swipe of her tongue, Damica wet her dry lips. Dorian's eyes lowered to latch on to the movement, further shrinking her self-discipline.

Urgh! He was her own personal cookie jar! She'd digested a few bites, but that wasn't enough. Her hunger wouldn't be satisfied until she'd devoured every single chocolate chip, crumb and calorie in the glass container. Her old hedonist ways had taught her that the label of the forbidden increased a person's appeal tenfold.

Ever the gentleman, Dorian averted his gaze from her mouth immediately and dispatched a friendly salute to the admin podium, where the receptionist and Ravi were waiting. He kept his tone hushed as he spoke. 'Would you be comfortable if we did...?'

He left her to fill in the blank. The missing chunk of his enquiry hung in the air, adding to the unbearable tension that had been increasing since...

She wanted to blame their kiss. But a frightening honesty with herself unveiled that she'd craved him—her best friend—since their heart-to-heart on the waterfront. Their first evening together at the resort.

Unflinchingly, she confronted his considerate stare, and along with it the fortnight's worth of pent-up pining and self-imposed frustration. No more dodging, ducking and diving.

'I wouldn't be...*un*comfortable.'

To an outsider, it might appear that she was talking in code. But her subtext—of which Dorian was and had always been a fluent speaker—was loud and clear.

Damica observed the thin layer of hope brightening his eyes, like a film that had been restored to top quality. In lieu of pouncing on the opportunity, he looked deeply into her eyes for any hint of hesitation. His pause amplified the attraction she felt towards him.

'We can stop at any time. Just tell me and we'll get dressed...'

Reframing her perspective, she reordered the timeline of events leading up to her choice. What if last night on the beach hadn't been the catalyst but the final necessary step before taking a leap of faith. What if her feelings for Dorian weren't an obstruction, but actually a feature of her new life post-fame?

They were two single adults vacationing at a luxury holiday resort devoid of paparazzi. There would be no significant harm in giving in to the gravitational pull. Dorian had just broken off an engagement. A wife and kids probably weren't his primary concerns—and he'd never cast her as a wife. Damica would be able to have fun with him without forfeiting her freedom.

'I trust you.'

Adding credibility to her point, she placed her palm on his chest, gifting it with a light and playful pat. Her heart bounced in retaliation to the attack of arousal initiated by her simply coming into contact with his upper body. Likewise, the promise of more seemed to have outmanoeuvred Dorian's qualms, splitting his serious countenance with a slow-growing grin.

She beamed back at him. Her mind was made up and so was his. 'Come on, it'll be fun!'

CHAPTER TEN

DORIAN COUGHED, the display so hyperbolic it sounded as though he was on the verge of hacking up a lung.

'I'm ready for you now, milady.'

Any remaining flecks of Damica's nervousness were successfully sucked into the vacuum of Dorian's foolishness. She emerged from behind the room divider wearing the allocated spa robe, which was embroidered with Étoile Privée's world-famous logo.

'Shut. Up.'

Dorian gasped. 'Is this how you deign to treat a service worker at your beck and call?'

She lazily swung the hanging tie of her robe as if it was a lasso. 'If I find out you've been speaking to journalists about this, you're fired.'

Dorian's humour was a beloved tactic, but it was an ineffective distraction.

'Ouch! Worst boss ever.'

Laughter quaked through Dorian's exposed chest. The dark hair all over his torso congregated to form a trail that disappeared below his waistline. A fluffy white Étoile Privée towel sat low on his hips, acting as the lone preventative barrier to full-frontal nudity on his part.

Quashing the procrastination that was delaying the inevitable, Damica pulled at her belt. The bow at her midsection came loose, and she tugged the garment down her arms. The robe slithered to the floor, landing around her ankles in a pool of flannel. She wasn't just stripping naked in front of him, she was shedding a skin.

'Where do you want me?'

He reciprocated her steadfast observation, extending their stare-off until the atmosphere was ripe with yearning.

Dorian read her like a book, learning her body in as much depth as his humble eyes would allow. Their adoring shimmer highlighted the symmetry of her soft breasts. His respect underlined her differing skin tones. And his unbearable longing lapped at the tips of her erect nipples and the triangle of hair guarding the apex of her supple thighs.

Unable to move himself from her line of sight, Dorian signalled to the massage table situated somewhere behind her.

Tearing herself away, Damica ascended what could be more accurately described as a *bed*. She lay on her front, settling on the padded white surface and aligning her frame with the curved dips designed to accommodate her breasts and knees. She folded her forearms under the rolled cushion at the head region, and let her cheek sink onto the plush surface.

Dorian came to her aid and drew a covering towel over her lower half, inducing an enticing tingle that outlined the backs of her legs and the swell of her ass.

The retreating sun spared some light for the room, which was a spotless white-and-cream-themed space with a premium fibre thatch roofing. All the doors facing the ocean were wide open to hail the expanse of cerulean water and its fresh, salted tang. She'd seen the Indian Ocean more times than she could count throughout this holiday, but she would never tire of it.

Only Ravi, another recent staple of her surroundings, was missing. He was conducting his duties from the hallway, allowing her and Dorian to be truly alone together for the first time since reuniting.

At the stand beside the massage table Dorian ummed and ahed over the rows of bottles lined up in a display box. An unscrewing sound, a pop and then a wet spillage on her back enlightened her to the fact that he'd made a selection.

Confidently, his palms glided over her exposed flesh, distributing the oil's moisture from the peaks of her shoulder blades to the very base of her spine and then the firm muscles in her neck and shoulders. They moved over the soft slope and rise in the middle of her back. Again and again. Over and over. Leaving no inch of her skin untouched or displeased.

The contented throb strumming at her core aligned with the building tempo of her heart, and goosebumps were awakened by his tactile expertise.

'You're good at this,' Damica said sleepily.

His talents didn't come as a surprise to her, after having witnessed his deft fingers bringing life to his artworks over the years. And under his sure hands, right now, she felt unequivocally safe.

Dorian kneaded the dimples at her lower back, using his thumbs to treat the knots of stress. He leaned down to whisper playfully in her ear. 'And *you* are tense.'

The heat of his breath tickled her ear canal, and Damica found herself intoxicated by his personal scent—fresh bergamot and oranges with rich, earthy oud.

He was so close…

Now was her chance to tell him how she felt.

She started off vague, lifting her head to correct her tilted view of him. 'I've got a lot on my mind.'

'Care to share?' Dorian drifted away to the opposite end of the table to reposition the towel and work on her calves.

Was she supposed to just come out and say it? Read out the entire novel of tenderness and need and angst she'd penned about him in her psyche. She wasn't well versed in how these sorts of things went. Usually, her romantic exploits didn't require much: a quick You up? text at three a.m. or a provocative glance from across a club.

'I've been thinking about how much I like being here with you. Like…really, *really* like being here with you.'

No, that isn't right.

She cringed at herself.

The hundreds of emails she'd written to him had always come with the option to backspace and edit her deepest thoughts to her heart's content. In person, she was nowhere near as concise or eloquent. How she'd managed to condense her emotions into a digital message and a handful of emojis was a grand mystery.

Irrespective of her tongue-tied trip-up, Dorian seemed to be trying his best to understand her.

His fingers drew intricate patterns into her calves, heading nowhere in particular. Damica had never regarded that part of her body as erotic, but Dorian's fingertips seemed to ink whorls of pleasure into her bare skin like…like some sort of sensual tattoo.

'I enjoy your company too,' he said.

This heart-to-heart slugged forward at a torturous pace.

Dorian's touch encircled her ankle next, and her entire body seemed to hum in approval.

'Um…that's good…'

Who was she kidding?

Talking would achieve little. Actions would pass on the message infinitely better than words ever could. Knowing Dorian, she believed he was principled to a fault. The chances of him falling on his own sword were far greater than of him rehashing last night's lip-lock. Even more so when he factored in that she'd explicitly said he wasn't her type…

So what? Types were changeable…they weren't laws. What was she doing?

'Damica, what are you *doing*?' she chided herself out loud, breaching the limits of her rationale.

Dorian immediately retracted his hands from her body—which was the polar opposite of what she wanted.

'I think we should stop,' he said. 'I don't know what's wrong, but—'

Damica scrambled upward, so that she was sitting on the edge of the massage table with Dorian standing between her dangling legs. The scrap of modesty granted by the towel fell away, brunching around her waist—although she didn't care in the slightest about that. The elevated surface meant she had to lean down to get to his mouth. But he eagerly met her halfway, stepping deeper into the invitation of her open thighs and tipping his head back.

Their ready lips collided, forming the beginnings of another messy, imperfect kiss.

Damica kept her eyes closed this time, surrendering wholeheartedly to their shared passion.

With one hand, Dorian securely held the back of her neck, intent on keeping her close whilst he sucked and nipped at her lower lip. Needy for more, Damica yielded and bared her all to him. Everything she wasn't fluent enough to express through words.

Walking away from him at the end of this vacation would kill her.

Whether Dorian could actually interpret the exact contents of her confession was unconfirmed. But he might as well be reading her mind... The slow caress of his lips persisted, in cahoots with the slow, intimate flick of his tongue against hers. Damica moaned into him, equalling his fervour and clutching at the dependable width of his shoulders.

She almost teetered into a disappointed whine when Dorian tore his mouth away.

'Shh...' His forefinger connected with his swollen lips, then jabbed at the closed doorway. On the other side of which stood Ravi.

Dorian's irises shone with a daring glitter, and he shot her a conspiratorial smirk before bending his head to track more kisses down the path of her exposed neck. Her bated breath verged on another crescendo when he journeyed lower to worship her breasts.

His grip on her thighs impelled her to tighten her legs around him. Frantic fingers threaded themselves through his hair and her back arched, pushing the peaks of her breasts further into the generous lapping of his tongue. They were a closed circuit, and an electrifying charge pulsed through Damica, thrusting her pleasure-points towards explosive consequences.

Dorian momentarily came up for air, responding to her gratified sighs with a breathless smile. He wanted this too.

She chanced another peek at the closed door, imploring the heavens that Ravi wouldn't come bounding inside.

Dorian was lost in his reverence of her breasts, and a low groan escaped him. The mist screening Damica's already non-existent inhibitions thickened.

Adulthood had come with many lessons. The most resounding of them all being the realisation that, on occasion, her happiness was lodged in unexpected places. But she knew that, once discovered, she should cherish it with all her might. For as long as the time constraints of their private session would allow.

Her shaky touch roved past his gold chain, accidentally snagging on the metal on its way to his taut back. Dorian's high praise persevered without interruption, his mouth developing a new obsession with her collarbone. Damica's fingers skirted boldly along the frontier of the towel concealing his lower body and…

Fraught with anxiety, Dorian lurched away from Damica. Those captivating thighs locked around him gave way at his struggle. To make matters worse, his elbow rammed into the box in which the extensive array of massage oil bottles were stowed. The box plummeted to the floor—but not before jostling a neighbouring vase that housed a cluster of decorative white orchids.

Damica tried to save the vase, but it canted out of her reach and succumbed to gravity.

Its final fate was a devastating smash that made the china fragment into a dozen sharp pieces.

A timid yelp unlike anything he'd ever heard from Damica before pierced the air. She scrabbled around the massage table for her towel, so she could cover herself up.

'Your Highness…? Your Highness…?'

Ravi was checking in with him, maintaining enough composure for the both of them. Funny… Dorian had missed him barging into the room.

'Dorian?'

The temporary paralysis holding him hostage

was lifted. The first thing he noticed was the unpleasant stickiness binding his toes. Massage oil.

The crate was upended and its entire contents were scattered all over the ground. Poorly closed bottles—he'd cracked open a fair few to smell them earlier—had rolled astray, spilling liquid everywhere. The faux straw stuffing that had served as the objects' padding was now a dispersion of sad, soggy clumps that were beyond saving.

'Nothing to see here, Ravi. I got ahead of myself, that's all,' Dorian muttered, blazing in the flames of his humiliation.

Throwing a temper tantrum wasn't his style, nor appropriate for a man his age. But then again, how could he refer to himself as a man in good faith when he couldn't go more than half an hour without the supervision of a glorified nanny?

Damica, scantily clad in her towel, was helping the spa receptionist to collect and properly fasten the fallen bottles.

'Please don't worry, Miss Foye—I mean *Mrs Williams*. These kinds of incidents happen all the time,' the resort employee assured the group.

Never one to let other people clean up his messes, Dorian stooped down to assist with gathering the tumbled articles. Coincidentally, he and Damica made contact as they zeroed in on the same bottle. The aftermath of their tryst singed through Dorian, inducing a giddy warmth. However, Damica yanked her hand away as though she'd been scorched.

He angled his face strategically to catch her eye, but she kept her vision downcast, denying him at every turn.

What else had he expected? The commotion he'd caused had been so loud that anyone might theorise it was a deliberate act of sabotage. And they would be partially correct in thinking so…

Somehow his body had viciously divorced itself from his mind the second Damica had tugged on his towel. She'd wanted him to take it off, and Dorian had been highly in favour of the suggestion.

In his head only.

Averse to this idea, his body had shut down all possibilities of that happening. Because nudity would lead to sex, and sex would lead to him underperforming.

He hadn't been sexually active…not since receiving his semen analysis results. The doctor had spoken with him at length about his options going forward, and dispelled any myths about a low sperm count leading to impotence. However, that talk had been a mere blur in a previous lifetime, outpopulated by fear and stress.

If the human body was a temple, as the bible dictated that it was, then Dorian's wasn't in the right state to receive any worshippers.

190 PRINCE'S REUNION IN PARADISE

And Damica deserved the very best.

Now she dumped the last of the debris into the box, which had been reincarnated as a makeshift bin for the ruined goods.

'I'm gonna just…put my clothes back on. See you at dinner.'

The latter end of her hesitant announcement was aimed more at Ravi than him. Damica scooped up her spa robe—the last piece of evidence tracing back to her frolic with Dorian. Then she disappeared behind the dressing screen to recuperate from the whiplash Dorian had inflicted upon her.

Desperation ordered him to chase after her, to beg until she spared him enough time to adequately plead his case. Yet self-loathing had staked its claim, sealing him to his spot on the floor and holding him captive.

In this context, would she find his truth believable, or would she find his explanation too outlandish?

Dorian mustered enough poise to rise to his feet, and subtly he made sure the towel around his waist was positioned to remain in place. The material going rogue was both the last thing he needed and the last ingredient required to transform this already catastrophic ordeal into a full-on nightmare.

A hopeful intake of breath attracted Dorian's crumbling awareness to the mobile phone the spa receptionist was taking out of her uniform pocket. He knew what she wanted, even before she was able to finish voicing her ill-timed request.

'Mr Sotiropoulos—'

'Your Highness,' Ravi interrupted her with a clipped tone.

Dorian knew Ravi smacking the device out of her hands wasn't appropriate, so his trademark irritability would have to do.

'Sorry, Prince Dorian—'

'Your Highness.'

'My apologies… Your Highness.' She had the decency to appear contrite as she held out her phone like a beggar petitioning for pennies. 'Would you mind taking a quick selfie with me? My whole family—especially my mama—are massive fans…'

She recited a few impressive facts about the Concarri Youth Arts Foundation, the crown jewel in his charity endeavours.

'It would be my pleasure.'

Dorian parroted the standard response that he had delivered so frequently it was branded into his lexicon, and hoisted up the towel… loincloth…accessory to his vulnerability, and clamped his hand over the fabric, just to be on the safe side.

Functioning on autopilot, he shuffled to the

girl's side as she prepared her phone to snap a picture.

The shot was perfect, consisting of what Dorian classed as his 'model smile'—a feature of a thing, devised to be looked at. He was a national treasure with universal appeal and a beam fit for public occasions. When in private he didn't have much to smile about.

CHAPTER ELEVEN

IT CAME AS a surprise to no one that Dorian did not, in fact, see Damica at dinner. Citing exhaustion from the jet skiing, she kept to her villa for the evening.

Her correspondence with him was still active, albeit distant: the odd emoji in reply to selfies of him nursing a cocktail and pulling comically mournful faces to poke fun at his solo dining experience. But he'd take a solitary crying-in-laughter emoticon over painful silence any day.

She didn't mention the episode at the spa. And Dorian didn't push her to do so. As unfamiliar as their romantic path was to him, he knew her well enough to respect that she hated being smothered.

So he would wait until she was ready.

However, that didn't change how lonely he was. At the overwater restaurant, outnumbered by tables housing happy families, couples and friendship groups, Dorian was reintroduced to a feeling he hadn't undergone since that fateful night he'd asked Damica and Jalen to join him. He'd taken one miraculous step forward, only to flounder down a full staircase.

How beautiful could a paradise like Étoile Privée truly be without a partner of equal footing to enjoy it with? What use was a life with all the world's riches at his disposal if there was no partner or children for him to share them with?

His life was in no way a fairytale, but the similarities mocked him. Like a knock-off Pinocchio, no matter how much he postured and deluded himself into creating a more masculine mould, he would never be a real man. The setback at the spa was proof.

In spite of all this, Dorian was well acquainted with the notion of breezing his way through adversity. And with a brand-new day came a brand-new chance to convince Damica—and himself—that he was worth the hassle.

His text message didn't go unanswered. Neither did his request for her to meet him on the beach adjoining the Club Enfant clubhouse after breakfast. She showed up.

Jalen bounded ahead of her on the shore, while she hung back armed with her sunglasses and the protruding shadow of her parasol. If the boy's return was a tool to render Dorian defenceless, it worked like a charm. He sank to his knees in the sand, all set for when Jalen catapulted into his arms in a detonation of beach toys and chatter.

At the rate of a thousand words per minute, Jalen recounted his day away from Damica and Dorian, and Dorian hung on every detail.

The day's sandcastle construction project was well underway before he was able to slip away unnoticed. Without prompting, Ravi replaced Dorian, taking up an abandoned spade and shovelling the sand to deepen the moat engineered by Jalen.

Dorian moved over to where Damica was sprawled on a beach towel in the shade. Upon his arrival she tensed, but inched sideways to make room for him. He lay down, propping himself up on his elbow, hoping he appeared in some way suave.

'You were missed last night,' he said, testing the waters.

'So, your clawed friends decided not to stick around, then?' she mused quietly, referring to the crab and lobster spread he'd ordered for one. He'd joked about them secretly being still alive, and hatching a plot to run back to the refuge of their natural habitat.

'Quite the opposite…'

Dorian's gaze bored into the impenetrable lenses of her sunglasses, battling with his own distorted reflection. The dark mirrors inflated his forehead and diminished his eyes.

'Between my meal and Ravi's crabbiness I had more than my fill.'

Her commiseration was hollow. 'Yikes…'

'Yeah.'

Dorian's charm offensive was about as stable as a house of cards. He usually regarded all the literature he'd consumed about romantic love to be full of gross exaggeration. Artistic licence gone wild. Embellishment for the sake of art. But the unbearable silence between himself and Damica revealed the truth behind every cliche and then some.

Without the bright rays of her smile he was trapped in a rainy day, his heart was bludgeoning at his chest walls and he would gladly trade his soul to have it back.

Damica sat up to fish around in her bag, widening the distance between them physically and emotionally. She uncapped her sunscreen. The plastic bottle farted as she squeezed a blob onto her arm. The ridiculous sound only worsened the void dividing them.

He was losing her…

And he had a dearth of functional relationships to coach him through this.

His arrangement with Sophie had been that of two adults allied by lust and common charitable goals.

Outside of lambasting him for not taking part in any sport, Dorian's father took a one-size-fits-all approach to his son's rare pleas for general life advice.

Feeling nervous about giving a speech to the nation? Man up, smoke a cigarette and get over it.

Unsure what to study at university? Throw away those pathetic paintbrushes and man up.

Over thirty and still single? Man. Up.

The closest he'd got to genuine fatherly guidance had been Ravi's observation.

'You don't know what her reaction will be until you actually tell her.'

He could disclose everything—from the profundity of his love for her to his infertility diagnosis—and let the cards fall where there may. It was so simple that it was *scary.* As well as being the very antithesis of the manly ideal he'd been chasing to no avail. But all else was failing, and Dorian had little left to lose and Damica to gain by adopting a different strategy…

'About yesterday, Damica…'

Giving in to the mounting pressure, Dorian let his true emotions out of the floodgates. But seemingly, Damica had done away with her own restrictions too, resulting in a clumsy clash of speech from them both.

'Did I do something wrong…?'

'…for making you feel uncomfortable…'

'Heat of the moment…'

Dorian caught bits and pieces over his own incomprehensible babble about how much he hated this and didn't want to be apart from her ever again. Because he…he…

He fell silent, figuring he was grossly mishandling his revelation and would be better off lending his ear to her. When his turn to speak came around, he'd trust his own capability to speak about his infertility with patience and sensitivity.

You've lamented to her about fame, parental issues and the suffocation of human existence… why would this be any different?

Dorian struggled to calm his jittering nerves.

Damica neatly tucked her ankles underneath her body and sat on her knees, thoroughly rubbing the last of her sunscreen into the skin of her forearm. 'I know I'm not exactly princess material…' she began.

They circumvented the directness required for eye contact, instead settling for watching the recurring movement of her palm over her skin. Dorian was inundated with an awakening heat upon recalling her hushed moans in the spa and his mouth on hers…

'You're right. Princess material you are not.'

He laid his hand over hers, driving her to look at him. Finally. In close range, the transparency of her sunglasses exhibited the dejected droop of her wide eyes.

'But I'm in no position to shame you for that. I can't really be categorised as prince material either. When I said I was here on a sabbatical, I wasn't being truthful with you. I'm here to recuperate because I've received some news about my health… I might not be able to father children…'

Damica's face darkened a shade. Not with anger or repugnance, but because of the stranger suddenly standing over them and thus barricading the sunlight. Brightness rimmed the figure's silhouette and bounced blindingly off the glass screen of his mobile phone.

'Damica? Huge fan! Any chance I could get a photo?'

She conveyed her gratitude to the nameless fan, and politely declined the photo opportunity. But it was too late. The twosome's zone of safety was compromised. The insulated bubble in which he was just Dorian, and she was just Damica, was ruptured. This man—whatever his name was—was a storm cloud, tailored to bring a swift end to the sunshine they'd blissfully enjoyed so far.

'Oh, come on! One picture—just one!' The intruder shook his phone at Damica, sounding less like a fan and more akin to a press photographer.

His choice of holiday attire was inconspicuous…perhaps calculatedly so. Right down to the price tag still attached to his shorts. As though they had been purchased for the sole motive of blending in at the resort. It took a rule-bender to recognise a fellow rule-bender. Was this a paparazzi loophole to counter Étoile Privée's no-photographers-no-journalists policy? Checking into the resort pretending to be a guest…like some sort of Trojan Horse?

'What—too good for your fans now that you've got yourself a prince boyfriend?' the man went on.

Damica swerved the invader's incessant attempts to capture her in a photo, video, or any other pixelated format without her consent. Refusing to spare him an iota of attention, she promptly collected her bag and personal belongings.

'Jalen! Time to go inside, baby!'

Making himself useful, Dorian uprooted the parasol handle from its place in the sand and seized up the towel. In a shuddering heartbeat Ravi was by his side, to usher the Prince away from the scene unscathed. His allegiance lay with the heir to the Concarri throne and no one else.

'No…no…' Dorian veered away from his bodyguard's custody. He wasn't leaving. Not without Damica and Jalen.

The pap in disguise had wedged himself in between the child and his aunt. Damica had her hand splayed over her face as she tried to get around him, however he kept skidding into her path, intent on hounding the superstar into a headline-worthy outburst.

His frantic footsteps and belligerent questioning created an uproar of sand so petrifying that

Jalen curled up in a ball, clapping his hands over his eyes.

A compulsion to protect raged in Dorian. He marched over to the 'guest'—no, the bloodthirsty vulture.

'Hey!' he barked, serving himself up as a decoy.

The Étoile Privée resort was an oasis full of celebrities and high-profile clientele. But this particular hound knew he had struck gold with Dorian. Gluttonous for a scandal, he dialled his speculation up to a more obnoxious level. 'That your secret love child, Prince Dorian? Conceived before your...uh...manhood failure, Your Highness?'

Vexation, panic and blind fury bubbled over the tidily drawn margins of Dorian's brain. His sense of responsibility dictated that he fall back, let Ravi do his job, gather up Damica and Jalen and bolt to safety. Nonetheless, his baser nature—all the anger he'd spent nearly three decades squashing and suppressing and silencing—won out.

Evidently he was already an object of ridicule to this...this monster of man. Soon he would be a walking, talking spectacle for anyone who had access to the worldwide web. Far right commentators would make him their punch bag. Talk show panellists would gossip about him shamelessly. His father would balk. Advisors would talk his ear off about in vitro fertilisation, medical research, cutting edge treatment and so on.

This peaceful alternative reality at Étoile Privée, with Damica and Jalen, would be over.

If the time to say goodbye was upon him, Dorian swore to put up a fight until the bitter end.

'A prince with no balls, huh? Sounds like something made up by the Brothers Grimm!'

Dorian smacked the phone out of the imposter's grasp, sending the device somersaulting through the air. It landed meters away in the sand, demolishing the carefully crafted towers and turrets of Jalen's sandcastle.

'What the—? That's my private property!' the harasser complained.

The small window of opportunity available for him to point out the irony of this whinge quickly expired. Wrestling out of Ravi's restraining hold, Dorian raced to the place of demolition, where the photographer was scouring the crumbled sand clumps for his weapon of chaos.

Both men homed in on the hurled phone gleaming in the sand as though they were pirates tussling over legendary riches. Uninterested in playing fair, Dorian elbowed his opponent out of the way and kicked at the mobile phone with the technique of a professional soccer player. The pain erupting in his instep was cancelled out by his contentment in watching the phone fly off into an incoming wave.

'You've destroyed my property! I'll be sending you a bill for all damages caused!'

Playing the victim, the fake guest keeled over and gingerly touched his gut—the location where Dorian had jabbed him during their heated contest. In the eyes of their growing audience, Dorian supposed he did fit the stereotypical mould of a movie villain. Mothers shot him dirty looks, whilst calling their children over and holding them close. Friendship groups ogled his blow-up with raw bemusement.

What they thought of him, Dorian acknowledged, was out of his control. Never mind. It was Damica and Jalen's dignity and honour he was scrimmaging for anyway.

For a second time, Dorian closed in on the instigator of all this upset. Ravi inserted himself into Dorian's warpath, pushing him back and roaring commands to stand down. But his bodyguard's conflict defusion tactics were in vain. Still filled by his own wrath, Dorian determined to go *through* Ravi, seeing as he couldn't get around him.

He charged, dedicating his energy to ramming through six feet of rippling muscles, flesh and bones. As expected, he failed, and his imperious order for Ravi to move out of his way went disregarded.

Since clawing his way over the immovable bodyguard would be a pointless endeavour, Dorian hurled a caution over the human fence in front of him. 'Stay away from them or I'll… I'll…' His index finger jabbed at the air over Ravi's shoulder.

'Is that a threat, Your Highness?' the photographer queried at full volume—for his own benefit as well as for the viewing pleasure of their witnesses. He lifted his palms, leaning into his performance of surrender. Only the predatory shimmer winking from the very bottom of his hungry, pitiless eyes exposed his smoke-and-mirrors show. 'I just wanted a picture of your lady. I meant no harm to the kid. It was you—'

Hellbent on shutting the creature up once and for all, and banishing him to whatever dwelling he'd dared to scuttle out of, Dorian shouted, 'Stay away from my family! You foul, abominable—!'

'Enough!' Ravi whispered. 'I advise you to step away, Your Highness. If not for me, then for Jalen…'

The child's cries dissolved into Dorian's hearing and everything else—the end of Ravi's lecture, the photographer, the bystanders still staring—faded into oblivion. They were not demure sobs but wounded wails that suckerpunched Dorian in the throat, making him wobble backwards. Undoubtedly, *he* was the cause of such distress.

So much of his time recently had been assigned to licking his wounds and anguishing over whether he could conceive a child the traditional way that Dorian hadn't evaluated the thought of a child ever feeling proud enough to refer to him as their dad.

Right now, the prospect was an unequivocal thumbs-down. He was no better than his sorry excuse for a father, who was ruled by his ill temper without any basic compassion.

Once Dorian's hesitation presented itself Ravi pounced, slapping a hand down on his shoulder and directing him towards the beach's closest escape route. The weight of his talon-like clutch was irrefutable. Dorian couldn't wriggle his way out of this one, regardless of the context.

Damica's sun umbrella and towel lay on the sand in twisted shapes, like the casualties of a fatal crime. And their owner hugged her inconsolable nephew to her hip, trying to hide him away from the cause of the harm and vitriol that had led to their neglect.

Him.

CHAPTER TWELVE

ONCE UPON A TIME, when Damica had fantasised about inviting the Crown Prince of Concarre into her sleeping quarters, it had been in the lead-up to more pleasurable events. The current situation they were tangled up in was anything but that.

She left the bedroom door open a crack, so she could survey Jalen where he was sitting cross-legged on the living room rug, under the spell of his favourite cartoons. Ravi worked around him, amassing the scrunched-up tissues used to wipe the boy's tears and snot. Somewhere in her and Dorian's much-needed chat Damica planned to advocate for the security guard to receive a substantial pay rise.

Incapable of delaying the unavoidable for much longer, Damica took off her sunglasses and turned to face Dorian.

"'My family…'"?' She duplicated the wording from his meltdown on the beach, but went easy on the yelling of it out of fear that Jalen might overhear. "'Stay away from my…*family*'"?'

Dorian started to walk around the hastily made king-sized bed, then immediately retired this course of action. He stayed firmly in his own territory, near the sliding glass wall that overlooked the villa's swimming pools. Although his arms were tucked respectfully behind his back, his pose held more self-restraint than royal honour.

'Damica, I can explain…'

'Yeah, please do!' She chuckled uneasily, still comparing the irate mortal on the beach to the picture of civility before her.

'Uh… I love you.'

'Love you too,' she fired back casually. 'Always have.'

'No, allow me to clarify. I am in love with you—in every comprehensible way that one human being can love another,' Dorian asserted.

Damica said nothing. At the spa, in the thick of foreplay, she'd been ready for this. She'd been naked, writhing, basically offering herself up on a silver platter, begging for Dorian to take her.

And he'd spat her out as if she was a toxin.

Following his disclosure that he was having trouble with his…y'know—something that was clearly tough and burdensome—Dorian's U-turn made sense. But then the slate had been wiped clean and a new narrative had suddenly been in motion. One she hadn't been privy to.

While he'd screamed with such certainty that

she and Jalen were his family, Damica's confidence in knowing him wholeheartedly had diminished.

'So you meant "family" as in husband, wife and child. Not...not siblings or whatever. Good to know.' She dumped her sunglasses on the bedside dresser, just so her aimless hands would have something to do. Darkly, she added, 'Because I'm pretty sure brothers aren't supposed to play with their sister's tits.'

Normally being crude brought her little shame. In this instance, though, she almost choked on what she'd intended to be a droll and snarky comment.

Dorian's face was pinched with remorse. He was clearly aware that the severity of his misstep was leaps and bounds beyond simply kicking a pap's phone into the ocean. All it would take was one anonymous tip to a celebrity gossip publication or forum and their privacy would be gone. Nothing got people talking like a royal romance—especially the unconventional kind.

'That was a...a Freudian slip. Please accept my deepest apologies.'

Heading back towards her safety zone near the door, Damica grasped the door knob, as if dependent on the coolness of the metal. She was in danger of overheating...her brain activity was computing too many optics and requests, and...

The amplification of her voice dipped, to sever

all chances of her nephew eavesdropping. 'Keep them. Or, better yet, give them to Jalen.'

'I...'

Dorian's face was awash with grimness. Bringing up Jalen's well-being was probing a soft spot...and perhaps a low blow. But Damica's guilt for dressing up her true sentiments as the hypothetical hurt feelings of her infant nephew was only partial. Any surviving culpability was cancelled out by the fact that she was correct.

'We both know how this is going to go. When this vacation is over, you're gonna fly back to Concarre and marry a model citizen. You'll have about three children—an heir, a spare and an extra—via the latest fertility procedure that unleashes biological warfare on a woman's body. Then you'll toss Jalen aside like he was nothing—'

Out of breath, Damica cut herself off to recoup.

Dorian called her out flatly, before she could recommence her escalating rant. 'You're hiding behind Jalen.'

A minute bud of hope sprouted in the same place where Damica's childhood happiness had wilted.

Maybe...maybe he did like her for her? How else would he be able to read her like a book?

All the better to control her with.

She killed the shoot of optimism, yanking at its roots and detaching herself from such naivete.

Her denial was harsh. 'Am *not*.'

'Are too,' Dorian insisted, refusing to release her from the impassioned stare-off he'd locked her in.

She squeezed the door knob so tightly that she almost lost all sensation in her fingers. Suddenly the high-ceilinged bedroom was too small and the walls too constricting. They weren't in a Maldives villa, but a breathtaking dolls' house: Dorian's fictional dreamland. Every tale needed main characters for the storyteller to boss around, and in this story Damica was the cookie cutter girlfriend/wife/love interest/ mother of his imaginary children. To him, she wasn't a person, but rather a vessel enabling him to live out his fantasies.

The frantic shake of her head was useless in drying her welling tears. 'You…you don't really love me.'

'I do, Damica!' he exclaimed.

Oh, he wanted to get loud? She could get loud.

'Dorian, wake up! I am a single woman of childbearing age. You're a man, desperate for a family.'

She gestured at the door, on the other side of which Jalen still sat. So much for keeping quiet. Damica tugged the door closed, to at least muffle the contents of their argument. There was no way she was letting an almost-but-not-quite-breakup cause Jalen's loss of innocence.

Walking over to the bed, Damica speared a knee into the mattress and reached for the wall above the headboard, where she had exhibited Dorian's artful drawing depicting himself with her and Jalen. In light of the new information, she saw that what she'd initially interpreted as a sweet gesture was obviously the sum of Dorian's projections.

Her rushed hand resulted in a careless extraction that tore the drawing's corners, leaving tiny, jagged triangles of sketchbook paper and balls of sticky tack attached to the wall.

After fighting to stand up, she rolled the piece of paper into a tube and prodded it at Dorian, urging him to take his gift back.

'Please take it.'

'No, I drew that for you and I want you to keep it.'

'W-we're just temporary Band-Aids that you're using to heal a long-term problem. And when you discover we don't fit your made-up expectations you'll be disappointed.'

She despised the fact that her voice waited until that very moment to crack. She pierced her lower lip with her front teeth to halt its tremble.

Here we go again.

Damica buckled into her metaphorical seat

belt and gathered all her other protective mechanisms to shelter herself from incoming hurt.

Her past was repeating itself in the present, and she had the foresight to accurately prophesy how their 'romance' would cross over into tragedy. Back then, the Feir Channel execs and her mother had had big business plans for her—their family-friendly product—and there had been repercussions when she wouldn't bend to their every will and whim. This time around she could save herself from unnecessary heartbreak.

The real her—Damica Foye—could never match up with the fictional ideal that existed in Dorian's head. She could never be his perfect princess bride.

But Dorian's stance didn't waver, and the stubborn clench of his jaw grew more defined. 'There's nothing temporary about what I feel for you.'

'Look me in the eyes and swear to me that you're not using me and Jalen to live out a fantasy, Dorian,' Damica demanded, refusing to believe him. She tapped the roll of paper against her thigh impatiently.

The silence that followed spoke volumes.

Damica let out a guttural scoff, holding on to her stomach so she didn't keel over. His reaction was incredibly informative. But so what? At this point, if she didn't laugh, she would cry.

'See? Look, you can't even deny it!'

Dorian pushed a hand through his bedraggled hair in a poor attempt to smooth out the mess he'd caused. 'At the start I did—'

'Wow!' Damica's heart shattered. Having suspicions was bad enough, but confirmation was a death sentence.

'But I realised that wasn't fair to you. Or to Jalen.'

It was a strong finish. He'd pieced his tenuous reasoning together convincingly. However, the damage had already been done.

Damica's voice was flat and devoid of any life. 'I think we should stay away from each other for the next few days. I need time to think.' Time to add insult to her own injury. 'The media isn't gonna let me breathe when I get back home. Us being seen together is only gonna add fuel to the fire.'

'I love how rebellious you are...and how you stick out your tongue ever so slightly when you're concentrating on something very deeply. You have a spectacular way with words, and I love the way you make fun of me. I love *you*—not some archaic notion of what a woman "should" be!'

It seemed Dorian was fighting to restore the zest and sparkle of their connection. But the elephant in the room was only reincarnated into a larger, sturdier model that reminded Damica that this wasn't her or Dorian's first time at this particular rodeo. He'd ditched her before, when she hadn't met his goody-two-shoes standards. How could she be sure he wouldn't get rid of her again?

Seeing that she was unreceptive to his declaration, he strode over and held her delicately by the shoulders. She didn't dare look anywhere other than at the sorrowful chasm behind his inspection. Dorian was desperately seeking reciprocation…and she was giving him nothing.

'I will give up my crown for you. Anything. Just say the word and…just let me fix this, Damica.'

Now he was just throwing promises at the wall to see what would stick and make her change her mind. She didn't get it. Why place her on such a high pedestal only to knock her down later down the line?

But Dorian seemed genuinely distraught over her pulling away, which scared her even more. The trap he was setting for her was so temptingly sweet that it was too good to be true. Like all candy, his promise was overwhelmingly sugary and doomed to rot her. Dorian would resent her when she failed to match up to the kind of domestic bliss he hungered for…wouldn't he?

In her lifetime, Damica had endured a lot—too many unfavourable conditions. But she knew with certainty that she wouldn't be able to survive Dorian falling out of love with her. Just the thought of him hating her was petrifying.

'Damica…?'

This was too much. With tensions and stakes running so high, she was beginning to feel boxed in. The Maldives getaway was supposed to have been a new start, an escape from the scars of her old life. Yet now the Étoile Privée resort had become an air-tight bubble in which she was being forced to confront her deep-rooted anxieties.

Well…there was ownership, agency and power in choosing which battles she wanted to fight, wasn't there? She was in over her head with Dorian—perhaps the mature thing to do would be to back away.

Her panic subsided a little with this line of thinking. So she would go all in.

Say something—anything to get him to back off.

Realising that her mouth was uncomfortably dry, she swallowed nervously. She held Dorian's fragile gaze, respecting him enough to look him in the eyes.

'I need time to deal with…your…your junk being…broken,' she lied.

Her wording was clunky and ungraceful, but the implication was explicit.

She might as well have stabbed him in the gut with a sword.

She watched Dorian's composure splinter, revealing a preview of his inner turmoil and agony. It went without saying that his fertility complications would cause a lot of controversy with his father, the royal advisors and the people of his country. It must be eating him up inside.

The skin on Damica's shoulders dropped in temperature as Dorian let her go, removing his naturally warming touch. She turned and spun the paper tube in her hands, ashamed of pretending not to wholeheartedly accept his fertility status.

'Take as much time as you need,' he said. 'I'll be at my villa.' He was covering up his dismay with formal politeness. 'When...if you're ready.'

Dorian's reconstruction of himself was quick, but Damica was well aware that her comment had floored him.

Too ashamed to speak, she stepped aside, freeing up the route to the closed bedroom door so he could get away from her. Her movement was concurrent with his, and they were suddenly snared in an awkward shuffle in which they were trying to get around each other, but stepping into each other's paths.

They both surrendered, stilling to let the other person pass first.

Dorian sent Damica a tight-lipped smile that was far removed from his classic radiance. He seemed to be analysing the structure and contours of her face, as though committing them to his memory. Then he leaned in to press a tender kiss to her cheek. So tender that she was terrified she might break into a million irreparable pieces in front of him if he prolonged his exit any longer.

She hung on to the familiar smell of his sweat and his cologne. Bergamot and oud.

With a defeated tug, he gently reclaimed the drawing from her guilty fingers.

And then he was gone, slipping out of the bedroom, opening and closing the door with a subdued click.

You made the right decision, she told herself.

Closing her eyes, she exhaled deeply before taking an uneven breath. She prioritised the regulation of her erratic breathing pattern over wiping away the wetness dotting her cheeks.

Inhale for four seconds, hold for seven seconds, exhale for eight.

You made the right choice!

Then why did she feel so wrong on an atomic level?

CHAPTER THIRTEEN

BELIEVING THAT HE and Ravi would be able to continue their stay at the Étoile Privée Resort after the public spectacle he'd made of himself on the beach was wishful thinking. Yet Dorian clung to the edges and points of hope, as though he was a passenger on a shooting star. Present for a short while. Subsequently gone. In the blink of an eye.

The door separating him from Damica closed with a terminating click. Ravi shot to his feet, standing tall and rigid. Such formality exposed the fact that he'd overhead…

Dorian realised that he couldn't even refer to him and Damica's argument as a 'lovers' spat'. She would actually have to love him back for the word 'lovers' to correctly apply to them. Adding on to that, there had been nothing trivial about their impassioned debate. The noun 'spat' did not resonate.

His first taste of true romance had doubt-lessly been eventful. He felt as though he'd been chewed up and expelled. He wondered how on earth people in their right minds could so eagerly chase this devastating emotion.

'Dorian…can we go and get ice cream?' Jalen tugged restlessly on the leg of Dorian's sand-crusted beach shorts.

'I think it would be better for you to ask your aunt.' Dorian knelt down so that they could converse on an equal level, eye to eye.

'But you and Auntie Dami were shouting at each other,' Jalen pointed out with youthful disdain.

Dorian got the impression that his and Damica's split was a major inconvenience to Jalen's appetite. The child's simple view almost made him burst out laughing, despite his current feelings of ruination.

He did wince, though. 'I'm sorry you had to hear that.'

By the sofa, Ravi let his eyes dart to the villa door discreetly. Dorian knew what that meant.

Wrap this up quickly, Your Highness. We must vacate the premises.

'I love you and your aunt very much, Jalen. No matter what happens next, I want you to remember that.'

Jalen's confusion at this took the form of a pronounced pout. Nonetheless, he agreed to Dorian's request for a hug. He kissed the boy's forehead and held him protectively.

Damica was wrong. When he looked at Jalen, he didn't see a placeholder for the child he might never be able to have. He saw the face of a unique child, overflowing with adventure and demands for the world around him, who had a bright future ahead of him. But Damica had also been right… It had been unfair to pursue her and Jalen's company with the intention of using them as a salve.

He wasn't healed. In fact, he was far from it.

If Dorian wished to mend himself on a psychological front, he needed to learn to accept his infertility diagnosis. The summoning to do so was swift.

'I've just received a lengthy, angry voicemail message from the palace communications office,' Ravi gravely informed Dorian, once they had departed from the family's rented villa.

They had left Damica still sequestered in her bedroom, and Jalen with his head stuck in his blissfully ignorant world of animation and high-action storylines.

Ravi gave the Prince a succinct update on the fast-progressing aftermath of his confrontation on the beach. 'Someone was filming. They uploaded the video to a social media site.'

'How bad is it?' Dorian asked, although he could already foretell the severity level.

Astronomical.

Jaw clenching in irritation, the bodyguard thrust his mobile phone at Dorian. 'Here. I've lost all hope that anything I say to you will matter, Your Highness.'

OMG! Prince Dorian of Concarre has gone berserk!! #goodboygonebad

A shaky hand had managed to capture the infamous 'stay away from my family' line, and Dorian, Ravi, Damica and Jalen hurrying away from the scene.

The view count was climbing rapidly. But what crushed Dorian was the footage of him reaching for Damica's hand in an effort to portray a united front and her shifting away from him.

Ravi stuffed his phone back into the pocket of his sandy blazer. The two men marched down the connected wooden pathways, following the quickest route back to Dorian's waterfront villa.

'I must speak with the security team as soon as possible to devise the best strategy for your safety, Your Highness. That video is geotagged, and we are sitting ducks here at the resort with no extra backup. I know you want to spend more time with Miss Damica and little Mr Jalen, but we may have to leave—'

'And I will go willingly,' Dorian interrupted with a clipped tone.

Dorian and Ravi were standing in the main reception building bright and early the next morning, to check out of the Étoile Privée resort. However, the only light experienced by Dorian was that of the Maldives' natural climate. Sunglasses covered his twitching, unfocused, sleep-deprived eyes and he was tempted to rearrange his numerous suitcases around him to form a hut, and collapse within their enclosure.

'Thank you for visiting us here at Étoile Privée the Maldives,' the male receptionist said pleasantly as Dorian handed over his villa key card. 'We wish you and your companion safe travels.'

As though on cue, Ravi barked into the mouthpiece of his mobile phone. Something about how the car transporting them to the private airfield was moving at a snail's pace.

Dorian mustered up his finest smile, although a mournful jerk pulled at the corners of his lips. 'Thank you. May your day be delightful.'

He turned away just as an urgent yawn invaded his jaw. The automatic doors of the foyer glided open, prompting Dorian to check the identity of the entrants for the umpteenth occasion.

Not Damica and Jalen.

A silver-haired oil tycoon, whom Dorian had met before once or twice, meandered inside with his young wife and children. The youngest of the three kids cantered ahead to the concierge desk situated nearby and pressed belligerently on the polished bell. The patriarch took off his wide-brimmed hat and replied to Dorian's stare with a friendly nod and a self-deprecating roll of his eyes.

Dorian couldn't tell whether the child's constant dinging of the bell or the family's matching sun visors were the targets of this father's joking response. Irrespective, he found both elements undeserving of dislike. In fact, he was congested with envy.

'I also need time to deal with...your...your junk being...broken...'

'Being...broken...'

'Broken...'

The rich family went on their way, and Dorian wrestled with his self-pity. He wasn't broken. Damica hadn't given him the validation he'd needed so badly, though, which burned with the severity of a bayonet assault. All his preconceived fears had come to fruition right then and there. In her eyes, the deficiency of his sperm meant he was incomplete and fragmented, and there was no point in refuting her belief any further.

Those hours he'd spent drawing, encapsulating all her nuances, had amounted to nothing.

His outlining the hollows, heights and extremities of his love for her hadn't evoked a positive reaction either.

And he suspected that his spur-of-the-moment pledge to renounce his title as Crown Prince and Heir Apparent had been the final nail in the coffin.

If he loved her as he'd so boldly claimed— which he did!—then he was obliged to listen to everything she said. And she wanted to be apart from him.

He wouldn't defy her or read between the lines, or try and psychoanalyse her. But in spite of this Dorian had a strong hunch that she'd vetoed his bid for mutual love because she was convinced that he was just like her mother and all those Feir Channel decision-makers. By stupidly admitting to pigeonholing Damica and Jalen at the very beginning of his stay, Dorian had accidentally implicated himself in a far greater crime: a covert plot to control Damica.

That blundered confession had been all the evidence she'd needed. Dorian had seen no good in voicing this and prolonging their disagreement, so he'd let her go. He couldn't manipulate her into saying she loved him.

His hand delved into the pocket of his shorts and his fingers brushed the folded edges of the goodbye letters he'd spent the duration of his sleepless night penning.

He'd been telling the truth when he'd let her know that he would wait for her at his villa. But now, with Ravi, the palace communications office and his father simultaneously breathing down his neck, Dorian knew he was unable to stall for much longer.

Damica hadn't called him during the night, nor had she stopped by his villa that morning. There was no telling if she would come over the coming days. Maybe she'd elected silence to speak on her behalf.

Dorian would sooner have words speak for him.

The automatic doors of the reception building coasted open again. However, Dorian didn't bother to scrutinise the newcomer.

Ravi did. 'Finally,' he complained aloud. 'I thought you had taken a detour in order to go sightseeing. Would you like a drink now that you are here? Our situation is not one of urgency, after all.'

The new arrival was their driver. Registering the magnitude of Ravi's hostile and sarcastic greeting, the man made a beeline for Dorian's suitcases, bowed, then started piling them onto one of the silver luggage trolleys provided by the resort.

He apologised profusely. 'I am so very deeply sorry, Your Highness. I know any excuse I give you will not be good enough—'

Dorian put up a hand to curb the employee's incessant grovelling. 'All is fine, I assure you. Please...'

On this holiday he'd experienced a semblance

of normality in spending time with Jalen and Damica. The imbalance of power between himself and his driver was now…disconcerting. Suddenly being waited on hand and foot, to the point of worship, wasn't only extremely infantilising, it also felt wrong.

Under Dorian's orders, the driver shut up immediately and got to work, wheeling the trolley outside to the open boot of an official state car.

Although the vehicle was stationary, Dorian was metaphorically already inside it, cruising along and pondering over an intersection that would not be visible through the window. The road leading to Damica had been blockaded— and she'd laid the bricks and cement herself. The other route presented a lonely existence, fenced inside stifling tradition.

These two bleak options couldn't be all life had in store for him, surely?

Dorian revisited the concrete foundations of his life as the Crown Prince of Concarre. Red-blooded, patriotic, old-fashioned masculinity was one of the core building blocks. Nonetheless, the bombshell of his worrisome sperm motility had caused Dorian's world to come crumbling down. There was now a giant hole for him to crawl out of—to freedom, should he wish for it.

Proposing that he would give up his crown for Damica had been an insane amount of pressure to put on her, and an easy way out for Dorian.

What he needed to do was walk away from royal life because he wanted to.

He was not broken. The spotlight on his fertility status wouldn't result in his ruination. It was simply a magnifying glass over the workings of his body, and a vital chance for him to learn about himself. With such knowledge came the power to make informed decisions relating to his own health. It was a set of doors that would open up wider public conversations about male infertility. Dorian was the one in control.

But by no means did he feel confident about how to navigate whatever came next. He was only secure in his call for something new. A third avenue.

The driver deposited the last of Dorian and Ravi's luggage into the boot. After pushing the lid shut, he trooped around the vehicle and opened the back door for the Prince.

'Are you ready to leave, Your Highness?' Ravi checked with him.

Dorian strummed the corners of the pieces of paper in his pocket, undecided over whether he wanted to pull them out.

CHAPTER FOURTEEN

THE TIME HAD come for Damica to face the music.

'Jalen, slow down!' she called.

Unsatisfied with her rate, he'd streaked ahead towards their destination: Dorian's villa.

Moving her watchful eyes between the boy in her care and trying not to trip over her own two feet, Damica shifted through the crumpled and dog-eared pieces of paper in her hands. The sheets—decorated at the top centre with a tiny star with wings, the Étoile Privée logo— had been worn down by her restless fingers. Likewise, her blurry vision was symptomatic of the hours spent agonising over the wording and memorising paragraphs upon paragraphs of her own scribbled handwriting.

Less than twenty-four hours had passed since her faux pas with Dorian, but it might as well have been a century—and Damica was desperate to make amends.

Scraping at the wall that overlooked her bed was only so useful… Four small sticky-tack stains refused to vanish, as if objecting to the missing art piece. And Damica had further tried to tidy away the remnants of the volcanic afternoon by distracting herself and Jalen with ice cream. But their ice cream parlour visit had quickly devolved into an unforgiving interrogation.

Why had she and Dorian been shouting together?

Because…because he'd said something special to her and she hadn't believed he was telling her the truth.

How did she know he wasn't telling the truth? Did she have a mind-reading machine like the super-villain in one of the cartoons Jalen was obsessed with?

She hated to burst his bubble, but no, she did not have the power of telepathy.

Oh…well, could she and Dorian just make up and be friends again? Jalen wanted to go back to the beach and rebuild the sandcastle wrecked by that strange shouty man with the phone.

Damica had been tickled by her young nephew's lack of complexity. Inspired by it, too.

She didn't have any mind-reading prowess, and she didn't have a third eye that could see into the future either. Ergo, there was no definitive way to verify whether Dorian was deceiving her, or to know if any romantic relationship they had would really crash and burn.

Without meaning to, Jalen had bulldozed the line of thinking she'd so religiously been parroting to herself. All the pieces were now scattered into newer categories. What she did know versus what she didn't know.

Damica had three unquestionable points.

Point One: Since she'd come together again with Dorian, he had conducted himself towards her with a reverence that was consistent and stable.

Point Two: When he'd confidently listed the ingredients that contributed to his love for her, she had felt terror-stricken.

Point Three: She'd referred to his fertility troubles as 'broken junk', but she hadn't meant it.

Damica's arranging and rearranging and additional rearranging of her reasoning had kept her up for half the night. What had started as a basic record of her thoughts had turned into a fully-fledged written admission of her fright and her feelings for Dorian.

She *did* love him.

To allow dread to dictate her life meant that she was still being restricted and controlled. The very thing she didn't want. Dorian had never imposed any physical or psychological limits on her. Quite the opposite. For the entire time she'd known him, and over the last few weeks, he'd been an advocate and supporter of her independence. But he wasn't a blind follower either, and would call her out when they didn't see eye to eye.

Surrendering to the uncertainty of romantic emotion was the wildest and freest thing she could do.

Calling Dorian broken had been pure projection on Damica's part. *She* was the one who was messed up. So messed up that she couldn't fully appreciate a good thing when it was right in front of her.

She hoped it wasn't too late to make amends.

Just like when she'd attended all those music industry award shows, she'd pre-planned exactly what she wanted to say, so she wouldn't become a pile of disjointed, incoherent sentences.

By the time she joined Jalen on the doorstep of Dorian's holiday villa, the young boy was leaping up and down on the 'welcome' doormat. Damica placed a stilling hand on his jumping shoulder and signalled for him to knock on the door.

The impact of Jalen's small fist on the wood caused it to drift open. Damica's brow crinkled. Why was the door already open?

The droning suction of a vacuum cleaner me-

andered from within the rented home, and a resort maid stuck her head around the corner that
marked the entrance into the living room.

'Good morning,' she addressed them diplo-
matically. 'Housekeeping.'

'House…keeping?' Damica parroted, just to
make sure she hadn't misheard what the maid
was telling her.

The employee nodded patiently.

An eraser seemed to be rubbing over the neat,
precise calligraphy Damica had used to mentally
choreograph today's heartfelt reconciliation.

Dorian was supposed to be here, with a pen
tucked behind his ear and a heavily annotated
literary classic tucked under his arm. And Ravi
would be plonked in the doorway like some sort
of sacred Easter Island statue, devoted to the villa's main entryway.

'I don't get it.' Jalen's head ping-ponged between his aunt and the uniformed woman in her
fifties. 'Where's Dorian and Ravi?'

'I don't know…'

You don't know? You do, though.

'I'm sorry, there are no guests currently staying at this villa. I recommend visiting the concierge desk to check whether any messages were
left for you.'

Dorian had left without so much as a goodbye.

Damica's hip connected awkwardly with the

doorway as Jalen barged past her and ran out of the villa.

'Jalen, where are you—?'

Damica quickly uttered her apologies to the maid they'd disturbed and restored the villa's door to its slightly open position. Hopping out of her flip-flops and collecting them speedily, she bolted after her nephew.

Jalen was scampering ahead, but still firmly within view. Somewhere during the unexpected workout she scrunched her pieces of paper into a ball, ready to cast her unrealistic optimism in the trash.

Naive. Foolish. Gullible.

Those things were what she was. Dorian had played her, and that whole Nice Guy monologue, with its assurance that he would be waiting for her at his villa, had clearly been bull.

Suddenly a splinter of wood wedged its way into the underside of her big toe. Damica cried out in pain, the momentum of her velocity slowing down into a limp.

You deserve this, crowed a tiny voice in her head that relied on dysfunction. *Karmic punishment.*

What had she expected? That he would welcome her back with open arms? How? She'd rejected him on the grounds of his undetermined fertility…which was scathingly personal. Every person had their limits—even Dorian. Patience was like an hourglass. The supply of sand seemed endless, but eventually the last of the grains would spill through the gap and no time, nor sand would remain.

Damica had run out of chances, and there was no option for a redo.

She hissed in discomfort as she extracted the splinter from her tender skin. When she had recovered, she managed to spot Jalen vanishing into the Étoile Privée reception building.

Damica hobbled through the parting automatic doors, luxuriating in the cool of the air-conditioned space. She closed in on her target: Jalen, in the queue of guests at the concierge desk. He was currently second in line.

'How many times do I have to tell you to stop running off, huh?' Damica snapped at him.

The authoritative, ill-tempered bass in her voice was unlike her, but she was at her wits' end now. Clamping a penalising hold around his elbow, she pulled him towards the exit. She reserved her strength, hoping her no-nonsense demeanour would do most of the heavy lifting.

Silly mistake.

Jalen wrangled himself out of captivity and scarpered to reclaim his position at the front of the forward-shuffling queue. 'No!' he yelled.

'Jalen…' she cautioned. 'You have three seconds to get over here or I'll…'

Do what?

She was only role-playing a demanding parent—although her frustration at the disobedient kid was oh-so-real.

Her nephew stamped his foot. 'I want Dorian!'

'Well, he's gone—and he's not coming back so…so get over it!' she shrieked. At herself more than at him.

They were causing a scene now. The very thing she *didn't* want to do. She was supposed to be lying low and doing ordinary things. Not falling in love with princes of foreign nations and getting involved in public arguments. Not being a poor caretaker for her family or having her hopes lobbed about only seconds before they were smashed to smithereens.

Holidaying at Étoile Privée had been a grave misreading of her needs.

Damica's swimming tears smeared the faces of their audience into indistinct blobs.

Jalen was up next at the concierge desk. He bounded up to the flawlessly polished counter and asked outright, 'Have you seen my friend Dorian?'

Wetness streaked the back of Damica's hand as she wiped her eyes. She walked unevenly to the concierge desk and quietly queried the attendant as to whether any messages had been left for her. She gave her full name and villa number—for show rather than diligence.

With a downcast stare, she distracted herself

with a meaningless analysis of the gleaming silver counter bell. The eager tapping of Jalen's feet made her stomach clench with angst.

Damica was already equipped to hear the employee say, no. Jalen, on the other hand, would be crushed. She'd tried her best to shield him from the devastation, but now he would have to live through it firsthand. Damica would do everything in her power to help him pick up the pieces…

'Ah, yes. One message here for you!' The receptionist whipped out a thin pile of folded sheets of paper.

A disorientating lightness overcame Damica, so that she forgot she had arms, and her flip-flops, the screwed-up paper ball—everything—nearly went clattering to the floor.

'There…is?'

The next interaction with the concierge was a blur.

Paper in hand, Damica virtually sleep-walked over to a corner of the resort reception area and collapsed. Jalen plonked himself down next to her, fussing over the written correspondence in Damica's grip.

'What does it say? What does it say?'

After a while, his fickle attention span migrated to the ball-shaped mass of paper composed of Damica's practised declarations.

Forcing herself to extend her curt, rapid breaths

into longer, more relaxing inhalations and exhalations, Damica opened the makeshift booklet.

Comfort spread over her taut chest when she saw the abundance of lines written in Dorian's orderly, looped handwriting.

He'd left her a letter.

Dear Damica,

In the wake of everything that's happened between us...every stutter, every blunder and mishap...it's fitting that I return to the way in which you and I communicate with each other best. The written word.

Let me start off this letter by clarifying: if you are reading this, I am likely no longer staying at the Étoile Privée resort. Ravi has informed me that it would be dangerous to remain in residence after my latest exploit.

I know I would deeply regret exposing you and Jalen to any more harm, so I have made the difficult decision to depart the Maldives and return to the royal household in Concarre. Please believe that it was my intention to wait for you at my villa until you were ready for us to discuss the scope of our feelings.

Whilst we may be physically parted, I hope that an emotional convergence of some sort can take place between us, if you wish.

When I first laid eyes on you, twenty

years ago, in that stuffy maintenance closet, I fell truly, madly and deeply in love with you. It was, and still is, a love full of friendship and great admiration.

Before you, I did not know what it meant to have a confidante who made me feel unequivocally safe and cherished. Who would entertain my tedious rambles about Monets and Klimts. Who understood the endless burdens of growing up under such an unrelenting public microscope.

I desire to bring you this kind of stability tenfold—not to satisfy my own ego, but because this is simply what a friend should do. My romantic regard of you is admittedly a newer and unfamiliar development, but I trust the foundation that we've built together.

If our splendid time together at Étoile Privée has taught me anything, it's that pleasure sometimes lies on the other side of risk. Whether exploring each other intimately, running through a Maldivian jungle, or hiding in closets, I would like you to be my partner, Damica.

I recognise how unfair and unjust it was of me to project my insecurities onto yourself and Jalen. Along with my appreciation, please see my apology. Swearing to forfeit my title in exchange for your love was a gross display of my desperation and a grave misinterpretation of your character.

Again, your fierce independence is one of your many inspiring traits. I failed you by treating your mind like something that could be easily swayed. Furthermore, I accept that whilst I aspire to be a recipient of your love, I cannot place any responsibility on you to affirm my manhood.

That task begins and ends with me.

What exactly will come next, I am unsure of. But I am confident that I have loved you for so long that I do not know how to go on without caring for you.

The media wildfire I have caused has ruined the possibility of a slow and peaceful meeting in the outside world, so I will keep my distance from you. There are plenty of matters for me to attend to in the meantime, the most urgent being whether my future is compatible with that of my nation.

A year from now, if there is any room in your heart for me, I would very much like to visit.

For ever and always yours,
Dorian
PS Please give Jalen a hug for me...

Damica shifted through the pages, rereading her favourite phrases and deriving new meanings from others.

There was an extra sheet at the back, which she assumed contained additional paragraphs of Dorian's words. However, upon closer inspection she found a well-known picture: the drawing of herself, Jalen and Dorian. Damica beheld its familiar aspects—Dorian lifting Jalen, whilst devoting himself to her—and visually digested the new.

An assembly of crease folds ran through the paper, and the shading was beginning to smudge. Not to mention the torn off corners. This image was less picture-perfect family and more...*real*.

At the bottom right corner was an email address that was undeniably a mature upgrade from mrdoryfish7@inbox.com.

The giggle puncturing Damica's throat thinned into a relieved sob.

Blindly, she felt around for Jalen and roped him into a hug.

EPILOGUE

One year later

DORIAN PULLED HIS bowtie loose, so that the silk-satin material hung freely around his neck. Blood circulation was restored to his head, and his shoulders relaxed when he undid not one, not two, but three buttons at the top of his dress shirt.

The red carpet for the Man of the Year Awards carried on uninterrupted, and Dorian took a moment to treasure the simple luxury of adjusting his uncomfortable outfit without having to consider the Concarri Royal Code of Conduct.

He followed his assistant to where the next interviewer was waiting with a microphone, a camera person and an ambitious smile.

'The night is young here at the Man of the Year Awards in Los Angeles! And I'm honoured to be joined by none other than His Grace Dorian Saadoun Sotiropoulos, Duke of Mirenz. Your Grace, you are set to receive the Gamechanger Award tonight—how are you feeling?'

Dorian was a picture of gallantry, in spite of the microphone being plunged into his face. 'Blessed...truly...'

Whilst some aspects of Dorian's life had changed beyond recognition, others remained the same.

After his speedy departure from the Maldives to Concarre, he'd booked a lengthy appointment with his father. As expected, the King had branded his son 'weak', 'insolent', and every other synonym for 'less than'. Instead of shrinking in the face of such abuse, as his reflexes had demanded, Dorian had stood his ground.

Renouncing his title as the nation's prince, publishing a memoir and partnering with a health charity to create a campaign focusing on men's infertility had been a wholly improvised reinvention. But Dorian had committed himself to making this rough design a reality over the last twelve months. In truth, he was still a work in progress, but overall he was lighter without the crippling pressures of prince hood.

All businesses had a PR front, and the royal family of Concarre was no different. The official statement it had released expressed sorrow over Dorian's decision to 'take a step back', and wished him the best in his upcoming ventures. He was no longer the Crown Prince, heir to the Concarri throne. He was now a lower-ranking duke—essentially a made-up title to help soften the blow of his monumental choice and leave the door open should he ever want to return.

A jeweller was only as profitable as his diamonds. Although he would have preferred a complete severance from his royal lineage, Dorian was willing to make this compromise. However, being called 'Your Grace' was still grating to his ears.

Halfway through the PR response he'd created with his assistant, Dorian became aware of his interviewer's slipping attention. 'I'm not boring you, am I?' he jested.

'No, Your Grace! Not at all!' The interviewer laughed. Looking straight down the rolling camera, he said, 'But it wouldn't be an award show without a jaw-dropping entrance!'

Damica wasn't supposed to be there.

She prided herself on being a rule-breaker, but feeling out of place at a red carpet for a men's achievement awards ceremony was only natural. Strutting along the stretch of scarlet fabric, she acted as if she owned the place.

The late summer night whispered against her bare knees, which were unabashedly exposed by her artfully ripped jeans. Gossipy breaths and greedy camera clicks bombarded the air. Images coasted along her eyeline like kaleidoscopic clouds. Nonetheless, her vision was narrowed down like binoculars, seeking one person in particular, and exhilaration coated her tongue.

Life after the Maldives had been constructive, healing and…*boring*. She'd done the right thing by going back home, keeping a low profile and scheduling an appointment with her therapist.

She had expected to receive a figurative pat on the back from the psychological professional. But just the reverse. The sixty-minute session had triggered a deeper dialogue about what she'd like to do now that she was no longer working in entertainment. The Maldives getaway had been a great starting point, but there was still work to be done concerning the reconstruction of her identity.

Who was Damica Foye?

Damica still didn't have an answer. She was learning to accept that finding herself was a life-long process, and that in order to unlock new dimensions of her personality she would have to try different things.

She'd dabbled in gardening, online history classes and archery—all of which she'd sucked at. But when it came to knitting and sewing, she'd displayed some promise. Designing and making a winter hat for Jalen had been a rewarding project.

Being in a stable, loving relationship was another experience she had been willing to try. And now Damica was feeling the fear and doing it anyway. At the twelve-month mark she had got in contact with Dorian again and they'd taken up a slow correspondence. Nothing had been on the table—they were just two people emailing back and forth.

And now, knowing Dorian as well as she did, Damica was prepared to initiate what they both wanted so badly.

At last, she spotted him.

Dorian—all the way at the other end of the carpet.

Their eyes met in a sustained hold, through the haze of people darting everywhere.

Damica watched him excuse himself from the interview he was taking part in with a contrite bow of his head. Her stride quickened in conjunction with her pulse—for a good reason this time. On the Étoile Privée beach Dorian had boldly proclaimed that she and Jalen were his, but she'd shied away from being publicly associated with him. Now it was her turn to proudly—and spontaneously—assert her love for him.

Narrowly avoiding a collision with an event usher guiding a boy band through the throng, Damica limboed and shimmied her way to the midpoint of the red carpet. Dorian had slowed to a stop, tuning out the assistant who was buzzing over his shoulder.

Their nervous smiles and absorbed eyes did most of the talking as they stood together for the first time since their torturous parting in the Maldives. She soaked in the rakish spin of his dapper suit: the undone buttons, loose tie, the single earring dangling from one lobe and the chunky rings adorning his fingers. And she knew he was admiring the springy curls of her natural hair all the way down to her sneakers.

'A-are you sure this is what you want?' he checked, breaking their embargo on speech.

Tears of happiness sprang to her eyes as she gave him a small nod.

She understood now that being in control wasn't a guarantee that she would always feel confident. Nonetheless, she was here as the main character in her own destiny. Whether her happily-ever-after with Dorian lasted for six months or six decades, she was choosing to do this with him.

They came together with a cathartic kiss. Dorian's affectionate hands cradled the back of her neck whilst their lips made love. She quivered under the thorough caress of his mouth and the lick of his tongue. Her own touch raked feverishly through his long hair, hanging on to his body for sustenance.

Every watchful eye and camera lens zoomed in on them, and a sea of flashing lights rose up…

The name Étoile Privée LA had a better ring to it, but the bedsheets were just as crisp there as in the Maldives location.

Having already abandoned her shoes at the door of the hotel suite where Dorian was staying, Damica tugged down the zipper of her jeans.

'Are you sure you're not going to get in trouble for skipping the ceremony?'

'They can send me the award by post.'

Dorian wormed the final button of his dress shirt out of its hole and flung his clothing onto the bedroom's Persian-style rug. Sitting on the edge of the awaiting California king-size bed, he snaked an arm around Damica's hips. Once she was standing between his open knees, he hooked his thumbs around both Damica's denim waistline and the lace of her underwear, then pushed the garments down.

Whilst undressing her, Dorian joked, 'Since when did you care about being well behaved?'

'Since being a fully-fledged adult with hobbies now, remember?'

Damica held on to his shoulders for balance as she stepped out of the jeans and kicked away the pesky material restraining her ankles. Dorian lifted the hem of her T-shirt and kissed his way up her abdomen in a line to her navel. Taking off her T-shirt and bralette, Damica giggled at his impatience.

Dorian put his mouth on pause to look up adoringly at her nakedness. 'Your fashion ventures? Yes… I think this is your best design so far, actually.'

She struck a playful pose. 'The Birthday Suit?'

'Yes…' Dorian gazed at her breasts, as if reliving their sensual massage session in the Maldives.

Damica bent down to trap him in another searing embrace.

Regaining awareness, and reciprocating the passion of her lips, Dorian hauled her onto the bed. Damica squeaked, bouncing into the mattress upon impact. They laughed together as he crawled on top of her and accepted the invitation between her spread thighs.

History was repeating itself, but Dorian was more confident this time around and there was no Ravi to hide from.

With his mouth and his tongue he relayed his devotion, leaving no area of Damica's body unappreciated. Bothered by his own state of half-dress, he stopped briefly to get rid of his dress trousers and boxers.

He kissed the crook of her neck. Around her navel. The backs of her knees. Up the span of her trembling thighs in pursuit of her core.

Every moan from her lips was well earned, and each stroke brought them closer together in ecstasy. The most intimate parts of her were on display, in a way that was new and invigorating for them both, but Dorian sank into the finer details and messy intensities. He held her open and applied an enticing pressure with his fingers until she shattered.

Afterwards, Damica lay in his arms, catching her breath whilst tracing patterns into his skin. She peered around the bedroom, through the extravagant drapes curtaining the large bed. 'I could get used to this...'

Dorian cringed at the sight of clothes and jewellery littering the floor like puddles. 'If I'd known you were coming tonight I would have prepared something special.' Keeping an arm curled firmly around her, he reached blindly for the phone on the bedside table. 'I'll order a room service meal for us. What are you in the mood for?'

Damica fiddled idly with a strand of his chest hair and smiled softly at the embarrassment tinging his cheeks. 'I like you like this.'

Dorian's reach fell dramatically short of the telephone. 'Mmm?'

'More relaxed. Ordinary. Normal.'

'I don't think we'll ever be normal, no matter how hard we try,' he admitted.

They shared a knowing gaze, ready for the consequences that waited for them in the outside world following their red carpet kiss.

A retired popstar and an ex-prince would always attract coverage—it was the natural way of things. The threat to her privacy would exist with or without Dorian, so she might as well tolerate the plague of locusts *with* him.

'We're as close as we can get, which is still a win.'

Damica remained optimistic, challenging her own negative thoughts and accepting that her lifelong struggles would not disappear overnight.

'I know that we agreed to take our time with things, but I need you to know that I don't want to do *this* with anyone else. I get that we don't have all the answers right now…about how to handle the headlines tomorrow or the best way for us to have kids. But I want us to figure it out together. Day by day, or much later down the line. I love you, Dorian.'

Dorian gave up his fumbling for the phone, his eyes alight with affection. 'The food can wait.'

'I told you I love you and *that's* what you have to say?'

'We've exchanged over twenty years' worth of words…'

Dorian rolled their bodies over, so that their legs were intertwined. Damica lay below him, gasping at the attack of kisses launched at her face.

Pecks rained down on her cheeks. He singled out her forehead next. 'Saying "I love you" back isn't enough…' Then her mouth. 'I have to show you.'

And he did.

* * * * *